DOWNSIDE UP

DOWNSIDE UP

RICHARD SCRIMGER

TUNDRA BOOKS

Tundra Books, a division of Random House of Canada Limited,
a Penguin Random House Company

Library and Archives Canada Cataloguing in Publication

Scrimger, Richard, 1957-, author
    Downside up / Richard Scrimger.

ISBN 978-1-77049-845-7 (bound)

    I. Title.

PS8587.C745D69 2016   jC813'.54   C2015-905752-3

Published simultaneously in the United States of America by
Tundra Books of Northern New York, a division of Random House
of Canada Limited, a Penguin Random House Company

Library of Congress Control Number: 2015954161

Edited by Tara Walker and Lara Hinchberger
Designed by Kelly Hill
Cover illustration © 2016 by Matt Forsythe
Printed and bound in the USA

www.penguinrandomhouse.ca

1   2   3   4   5   20   19   18   17   16

TUNDRA BOOKS | Penguin Random House

To my daughter Imogen, who helped me plot this one out. I was typing, she was jumping on the bed.

Love is strong as death
Song of Solomon

It wouldn't have happened if I hadn't been looking down. I think about that sometimes, what it means. Down. I was looking down, all right.

I walked out of school bouncing Casey's old tennis ball, like usual. Until Lance Levy kicked it out of my hand and I ran after it.

"Yesss!" Lance called. "See that? See the way I kicked Berdit's stupid tennis ball right out of his hand? Yesssssss!"

His voice chased me across the playground, then passed me, fading into the distance as Lance raced away down the street. He was the fastest kid in sixth grade. Yesss he was.

I was holding onto the ball when I came up to Velma Dudding, who was on the sidewalk in front of the school. I thought about saying hi to her. Or bye. Or see you tomorrow. But I didn't. Her mom drove up and Velma slipped into the front seat of the SUV. I walked on.

Izzy was waiting for me at the top of Sorauren Park.

"Hey, Fred," she said.

"Hey."

Now that I was closer to home I was bouncing the ball and catching it again.

"I changed my screen saver. Wanna see it?" said Izzy.

"Nah."

My eyes were on the ground. Cracked pavement. Weeds. Ants. Dirt. The tennis ball made a flat, hollow sound when it bounced.

"Come on, take a look. Harry has a new hat."

"Nah."

She's my big sister. Isabel. We both go to Sir John A. Macdonald Public School. She's in eighth grade, two years ahead of me. We cut across the bottom of Sorauren Park, crossed Wabash Avenue and headed down toward Wright Avenue. I bounced my ball off the paved path and caught it. Off the grass. Caught it again.

Izzy walked ahead of me. Her runners were broken at the back. The red heels flapped up and down. They looked like little mouths, opening and closing.

"Race you home, Fred!" she said.

"Huh?"

"Race you! Come on. From here to the back door. Ready . . . set . . . go."

I gave up after a few steps. She stopped, turned back for me.

"What is it?"

"Nothing."

"Give me your backpack. Let's keep racing."

She held out her hand.

"Nah," I said.

"Fred! This sad stuff is getting lame. Don't keep being a dope."

She grabbed my arm and pulled. I almost fell.

"Stop it," I said.

"Fine, be miserable!" She took off. I kept walking and bouncing the ball. I knew I was being an idiot. I didn't want to feel this way, but I couldn't help it. You can't help how you feel. I kept my head down.

The tennis ball took a funny bounce off bumpy ground. I ran after it. The ball stayed ahead of me, bouncing off garbage, stones, more bumps. It bounced over to a drain and disappeared.

No.

I didn't say anything, but that's what I was shouting inside. *No. No. No, no, no.* I went down on my knees. The drain was your regular city sewer grate—square with rusty metal bars. There was a wider space between the end and the first crossbar. That's where Casey's ball had gone. Usually a tennis ball wouldn't fit down a sewer grate, but his was bald from him chewing on it, smaller than a normal ball.

Pitch-dark in the drain. Pitch is tar, did you know? But *tar-dark* doesn't sound right. Anyway, it was really dark down there—and then a light flashed. Just a quick on-off, like your mom checking on you at night, opening and closing your door. I wouldn't have seen it if I hadn't been looking down. In that second of light, I saw Casey's ball, sitting on a concrete floor, near a puddle. I stared after the light went out. Like staring would bring the ball back to me. My heart was going bump in my chest.

Casey's my dog. Sorry—was. He was my dog. He died during March break. That was two months ago. I came downstairs for breakfast and he was lying on the floor by the front door. We took him to the animal hospital on Roncesvalles Avenue, and the vet told us his heart had given out. I wanted to know why.

The vet shrugged. "They just do sometimes," she said.

Mom put her hand on my shoulder. "Sorry, Fred," she said. "So sorry."

The vet said she'd take care of Casey.

"Take care of him?" I said.

"Yes."

"What does that mean?" I asked. "*Take care of him.* He's dead. You said so. How are you going to take care of him? Will you make him better? Will you cure him? Get him a new heart?"

The vet looked away.

"Fred." Mom sounded shocked. "This isn't like you."

I shook off her arm. "So you won't cure him. How will you take care of my dog, then? My dead dog. Will you bury him?"

I was crying now. The vet shook her head. She still wouldn't look at me.

"Time to go, honey," said Mom. She asked if I wanted to go for ice cream on the way home, which she usually doesn't. I said no.

I figured that when the vet said taking care of she meant burning.

Have you ever been sad? So sad you didn't want to talk to anyone. Or eat? Or get out of bed? That's how sad I was. Days and days. Mom made sure I got out of bed, and ate, and went to school. But I didn't talk much, after yelling at the vet that time. Lisa Wu started calling me Mouse—'cause I was quiet as a mouse, right? It was a joke. *Hey, Mouse, how's it going? Hey, Mouse, look, we got the same kind of sandwiches for lunch. You want to play, Mouse?* Lisa is a loudmouth, so I guess everyone is a mouse next to her. Dr. Nussbaum said it was okay not to talk very much. He said I'd talk when I felt like it.

A streetcar rumbled along Roncesvalles, a couple of blocks away. I kept looking down through the sewer grating. The weird light flashed again. Like a reminder. Casey's ball was still there.

You'd like Casey. He's a medium-sized black-and-brown guy who likes to jump and always looks like he's smiling. He's a good runner too. You should see him go. Sorry, was. He was a good runner. Was. He was gone, and now his ball was gone too. I wanted to get it back. But the grating was too heavy for me to lift by myself.

"You want a lever," said a voice from behind me. I turned. A teenager smiled at me. "A hockey stick or something to lift off the top. Usually these kind of sewers are just for storm overflow, but this one goes all the way down to the main line. There's steps and everything. You can climb down. I've done it."

I'd never seen this girl before. Where'd she come from? She had a long face and a nose that curved to one side. Her hair was white, like cake frosting. She put up one hand to scrunch it around.

"Do you *have* a hockey stick?" she asked.

I nodded.

"Well, then, there you go."

I scrambled to my feet and ran home.

I wanted to go right back to the vacant lot, but I couldn't. Mom marched me to the piano.

"Practice, young man," she said. "Fifteen minutes, starting now. You have a lesson in half an hour, and you've hardly practiced all week. At least do your scales. Get your mind off things."

"Yeah, things," said Izzy. She was across the hall in the living room, watching TV and texting. "Things like dead dogs," she said.

"Isabel!"

"I'm just saying." Izzy turned up the volume on her TV show.

I sat on the piano bench and put out my piano fingers. Curved, like claws. Miss Lea said this was the only way to play the piano. I found a D and went up the scale, hunting the right notes. White, white, black, white, white, white, black, white. And down. Up and down. I thought about Casey chasing his ball across the backyard, struggling to keep hold of it as I pulled it out of his mouth. You'd like Casey. He's a good dog. Sorry, was.

Up and down.

I didn't go to my piano lesson. I took my hockey stick from under the back porch and ran to Sorauren Park. No one was there. I found the storm drain and slid the stick blade between the narrow slots. I couldn't lever the grate up, so I rolled a big rock over and leaned the stick back against the rock. Now I had a teeter-totter with the rock in the middle. I pushed down on the butt end of the stick, and the blade end lifted the metal grating. I kept pushing down until the grating came right out of the drain and flipped over. It made a noise like a gong. *Clang-ang-ang-ang.*

Okay then.

I took off my backpack with my music book in it, twisted round so I was on my hands and knees, and slid myself into the sewer drain. I didn't decide to do this, any more than I decided to miss my music lesson. It was like I was acting on orders. I had to do it.

My feet found the metal rungs of the ladder on the wall, and I started down. The smell was water and mud. I lowered myself until I ran out of rungs. I was used to the dimness by now. Peering down through my legs, I could see Casey's ball, just a jump away. I let go and dropped to the floor. Only I didn't. Didn't land, I mean. I kept expecting to hit bottom, and I kept dropping. It was like when you are almost asleep and your legs fall off the world, and you wake up with a start. Only I kept falling. Around me was darkness. Seemed like I was falling fast. I was afraid to reach out in case I hit the side of the sewer and burned my hand.

I thought, *Am I dreaming?*

I thought, *Am I crazy?*

And kept falling.

I got used to it. You can get used to anything. I kept thinking I'd land, and I didn't and didn't and didn't, so I stopped expecting it. I saw another flash of light below me, like the kind I saw before. On-off. Just when I was starting to wonder if I would actually fall forever, I landed with a bump that shook my brains like dice. My knees telescoped up to my chin. I rolled over and over and lay still and thought, well, that wasn't so bad. Considering I'd fallen for who knew how many thousand miles, not so bad at all.

First thing I saw was Casey's ball, inches from my face. I grabbed it and squeezed. The feel of the thin fuzz and bald rubber brought me back to reality. I sat up and looked around. I was sitting on the floor of the sewer. Above my head was the metal ladder I'd come down, and at the top of that was a square hole showing blue sky—the sewer drain opening at the bottom of Sorauren Park. I hadn't fallen thousands of miles after all. More like a few feet. Weird or what? The whole falling thing could only have taken a second. I stood, put the ball in my pocket and reached for the lowest rung of the ladder.

I saw another flash, like the kind I'd been seeing, only this one was overhead, so I saw it looking up. Sun glinting off an airplane or something.

Climbing was no fun. I felt light-headed and pukey. Seriously pukey. The ride where the teacups whirl around does this to me too. Sweat on my forehead and hands. I took deep breaths because that sometimes helps. Popped my head over the rim of the sewer, and promptly threw up. Like pushing a button. No heaving and gasping, just *blatch*! I held tight to the top rung of the ladder while everything inside me came out.

I was upside down.

I thought I was climbing up out of the sewer, but it turned out I was climbing down to ground level. I had my head out of, well, the ceiling of the world.

That doesn't sound right—let me try again. You know the cartoon where they fall right through the world and end up in Australia or someplace, walking around upside down? Like that. Exactly like that.

I was upside down. No, that's not right. The world was upside down. Which is why I'd felt so pukey on the ladder. Why I *blatched*.

This wasn't Australia or China, like in the cartoons. It was my neighborhood. I recognized everything. The drain. The park between Wabash and Wright. The houses, the fences, the street signs. Everything just as I remembered it, except upside down.

I wasn't crazy—just sick. Something wrong with my eyes, my brain. That's why I felt like I was falling forever.

Still, it did look super weird.

My puddle of puke lay on the ground beside the sewer drain. I let go of the metal ladder for a second, worried that I might float away. I didn't. Gravity worked. I just had to get used to everything looking wrong.

Okay then.

I climbed slowly out of the drain, feeling lighter than normal, almost floating. I heard screeching and looked down—looked up, that is. I looked into the sky. Seagulls. I saw their white bellies, yellow feet. I couldn't understand. I was upside down and right side up too. Right side down.

The world spun. I vomited again, and again my sick fell upward to the ground. The world spun some more. I closed my eyes and put my hands over my ears.

Was I dreaming?

But you don't throw up in dreams. You don't smell how bad it is, don't feel the burning on the inside of your throat and nose. So this was not a dream. I really *was* sick. I fell and hurt my head, and now I was sick. *Home*, I thought. *Must get home.* I walked carefully, eyes level, afraid to look down or up. My steps were slow; my feet taking a long time to get down to the pavement.

Home. I went right to my room and lay on my bed. The ceiling below me spun around and around. I closed my eyes.

"Freddie?" said Izzy.

I squinted. She stood in the doorway.

"What are you doing here?" she said. "I saw you outside a minute ago."

I moaned.

"You sick? Aw, poor baby brother."

Usually Izzy made fun of me, but she sounded sort of serious here. Jokey, but she meant it.

"You don't look too good and that's a fact," she said. "Do you have a headache? Do you want me to bring you a cold cloth or something?"

Also, she hadn't said anything about me not going to my piano lesson. Also, she was calling me Freddie. Everybody calls me Fred, always has. Weird.

I shook my head, no.

"Okay, I'll go away. Hey, I like your shirt," she said. "Were you wearing that before or did you change just now? I don't think I've seen it. It's cool."

I was wearing my blue sweatshirt. I've had it forever. Since last year. I wore it to school today. I wear it a lot. Izzy has seen it a hundred times. A thousand.

"And look who's come to see you, Freddie!" she said. "Maybe he'll make you feel better, hey, boy?"

She held the door open so he could come in.

Casey.

2

I was out of the bed in a flash, falling forward, tripping across the floor to wrap my arms around him.
My dog. He barked, just once, quietly, like he does.
He stayed still, letting me hold him. I was on my knees
with my arms around him. I had my head buried in his
soft, dark fur. I could feel his warmth, feel him panting,
feel him.

Casey.

It was him, all right. My dog. The thing I missed
as much as I'd ever missed anything. More. He licked
me and I could feel his rough tongue and smell his dog
breath. It was just like all the other times he had licked
me. Just like.

I said his name over and over. I was gulping and
saying his name and gulping some more. *Case*-gulp-*y,
Case*-gulp-*y.*

I don't know how long I knelt there, holding him,
saying his name. It must have been a while, because he
got restless and whined. I didn't want to let him go. I

was afraid I'd wake up from my dream, and when I did he'd be gone.

He finally had enough and wriggled out of my arms. He shook himself and stretched, found the patch of afternoon sun in the middle of my carpet and lay down in it. He put his head on his paws and smiled over at me, showing his chipped tooth.

I didn't wake up. He didn't disappear.

I sat on the floor next to him, still feeling lighter than I had in a long time. Now that I figured I was in a dream, the upside-down thing made sense. Last week Mom told me about an experiment where they fitted a guy with goggles that turned the world upside down, and he got sick and disoriented, but not for long—in, like, no time at all his brain sorted out the images, flipping everything he saw the other way round, so he could wear the upside-down glasses and the world would look right side up. *Your brain is amazing*, Mom told me. *It can do anything!*

I must have been thinking of this when I fell asleep.

The world didn't look upside down anymore. The floor was under me, and the ceiling was over me. I didn't feel sick either. Not a bit. I stroked Casey. He went to sleep and I waited for the next part of the dream. The numbers on my bedside clock ticked over, 5:10, 5:11. Casey slept, and I sat on the floor of my room, and nothing happened. I was happy but puzzled too. You know how dreams work. You're flying, and then you're eating pizza, and then you're in a cave, and then you're in the bathtub wearing shoes, and then you're kissing Velma Dudding. What I mean is that dreams move fast. So as I sat here in my room with my dog, and nothing happened, I got to wondering what kind of dream this was.

I heard voices outside my room. One of them was Mom's.

"There you are," she said. "Izzy told me you were sick."

"Nope, I'm good," said the second voice. "But thanks for asking."

"I was just coming up to your room to check on you."

"That's real nice of you. But I'm feeling fine."

"Okay then. Love you, goofy boy!" said Mom with a chuckle.

"Love you too!"

My door handle turned and there he was. I hadn't recognized his voice, but I sure recognized *him*. I scrambled to my feet. We stared at each other. I don't know which of us was more surprised. Me, or me.

Yeah.

I might as well have been staring in a mirror. We were identical. Height and build and hair and eyes. I have a little thing on my chin—a mole. Him too. My hair won't stay straight and flops over my face. His too. I have a—well, all the things I have, he did too. I didn't own a gray hoodie like the one he was wearing, but I could have. It's my kind of thing to wear. I had one a couple of years ago.

He recovered quicker than me. He blinked and then broke out a big smile. I was trying to fit puzzle pieces together. "You know, you look just like me!" he said. "Are you my long-lost twin? Or are you me from another time? Is that it? Are you from the future? Is there time travel, and you've come back to visit? No, wait—you look the same age as me. You can't be future me unless they're going to invent time travel next month or something. So are you, like, my son from the future? Maybe that's it. They cloned some DNA of mine a hundred years from now, and you're the result. Gee, do they still wear sweatshirts in the future? And what are you doing in my room, patting my dog?"

"*My* dog!"

The words popped out. I didn't mean to be so loud. "My dog," I said again, quieter. Casey wagged his tail in his sleep.

I was sure I'd wake up now, but I didn't.

The boy asked me my name.

"Fred."

"Short for Frederick?"

I nodded.

"Frederick Berdit?"

I nodded again.

"Me too," he said.

We compared. We were both named Frederick Melvin Berdit, both with birthdays on May 21. Both in sixth grade. Both living at the same address on Wright Avenue in Toronto, Canada. Both with a sister named Izzy and no brothers, and a dog named Casey—only mine was dead.

We stood back-to-back and felt the tops of our heads. We were the same height. We compared arm length and shoe size. Exactly the same.

"So you're not from the future," he said. "Too bad. That would have been cool. Mind you, this is pretty cool too. You're some kind of identical twin, eh?"

I didn't know. I didn't know at all.

"The only difference is that you're Fred, and I'm Freddie."

"That's what Izzy called me," I said. "She thought I was you."

"Maybe that's it," he said.

"What?"

"You are me. I am you. Yeah." He nodded, snapping his fingers. "Yeah, that's it. That must be it." Talking even faster now. "Don't you get it, Fred? You're me from another world. A parallel place. This is so cool. Don't you think it's cool? Don't you? Hi there, Fred. Hi there, me. Great to meet you!"

He reached out and put his arms around me. He hugged me. I am not a hugger. I patted him on the shoulder.

"Parallel?" I said.

"Doesn't it make sense to you? We're identical and yet different. You're wearing a blue shirt. Your jeans are wet at the bottom."

I looked down.

"And you don't talk much," he said. "People say I talk all the time, they're always telling me to quiet down, but you hardly open your mouth. See? Like right there if I had been you, I would have said something. But you just stared at me like a fish. Ha ha, just kidding. You don't look like a fish. I mean, no more than I do. This is great! You're not me, but you're just like me. So I figure you must have come through some kind of portal and ended up here. You hear about parallel universes all the time, and that's what always happens. Someone finds a portal."

Casey stirred in his sleep. I went over and patted him. He smelled like himself. My dog.

"This could be a dream," I said.

"Huh? I don't see how we could both be dreaming

the same dream at the . . . Oh," he said. "You mean that I would be part of your dream. That I wouldn't be real."

I nodded.

"Oh. Yeah. Me not being real. Ha ha. That's kind of neat. How about it? Nah, I'm real. What about you, though? How do you know *you're* real?"

He came over and tickled me under the ribs.

"Does that feel real, Fred?" he said. "Or like a dream? Am I real? Am I?"

I pushed him away. "Stop!" I said. "Stop, Freddie!"

"Okay then," he said.

This made me jump. I say that too. Okay then.

"If it was a dream, would it be a good dream or a bad dream?" he said.

And now, darn it, I started to cry.

Not a gulp or a *hoo hoo,* no noise at all, just suddenly there were all these tears. He asked what was wrong. And I explained everything to him—falling, climbing out of the drain and finding everything was upside down, going home. And finding Casey.

"I *knew* it!" he said, pounding his fist into his palm. "I was right! Another world. An upside-down world! Wow!"

He took a deep breath. "And Casey's dead? In your world?"

"Yeah."

"Man, that's awful! But look, Fred." His eyes were bright as buttons. "Isn't it great that you found Casey here? I mean, this is real. But it's like living inside a good dream. Right?"

Casey rolled over so I could give him a tummy rub. He didn't feel like a dream. Or smell like one. What Freddie said made sense. Well, sense is the wrong word, but you know what I mean.

"So you lucked onto this drain, this . . . portal to an upside-down world!" he said.

"I was looking down," I said. "And there was this flash of light."

"That is so cool!" He waved his hands around. "And you didn't end up in Wonderland, or Oz or Narnia. You ended up back home. Way cooler! And is your place really just like this one, Fred? Do you have streetcars on Roncesvalles, and Kraft Dinner, and dragons, and Blue Banana jeans, and a science project with Velma?"

I looked up from rubbing Casey. "Velma Dudding?" I said.

"Yeah. Do you know her too? Are you in class with her? Miss Pullteeth's class, 6D? Velma and I are doing the water cycle together. Are you?"

"We don't start the water cycle til next week," I said. "But the rest is the same."

Velma sat in front of me. She had dark hair, star-tling eyes and bra straps I could see through her white shirts. I could never think of anything to say to her. I wondered if I'd get picked to work with her. A science project with Velma? Wow.

"What do you mean by dragons?" I said. "Is that your basketball team? Ours is the Raptors."

"Ours too," he said.

Before he could say anything more, we heard a knock on the door.

"Freddie?"

Mom's voice.

3

He put a finger to his lips.

"What's up, honey?" Mom called through the door.

We stared at each other. This was a secret and Mom was a grown-up. *Don't tell* is an imprinted code, part of kid DNA. The door handle turned. Freddie pointed under the bed and I dove. I trusted him—after all, he was me. Also because he was such a take-charge person.

"Come on in!" he called.

I heard the door open. I turned my head and saw my mom's running shoes. Same as the ones she wears at home.

"I made you a cup of tea," she said.

"Aw, Mom! You're the best. Thanks!"

"Yes I am!" she said with the second chuckle I'd heard from her. Which was two chuckles more than I'd heard from my mom in I didn't know how long.

"Coming upstairs just now I heard you talking to yourself," she said. "What was that about?"

"To myself?" he said. "Yeah, that's what I was doing, all right."

"There was something about dragons. Did you see one?"

"No, no. Just talking out loud and then answering myself. Conversation, you know?"

"You are a goof!" she said. "A real goof. Where do you get that from?"

"I wonder," he said, and they laughed together.

"So Mom heard us talking," I said. "But why did she think it was just you? I don't sound like you."

"Ever hear a recording of yourself, Fred? I have. I didn't recognize myself at all. You don't realize what you sound like to other people."

He slurped. His mug had a picture of a dog on it. Maybe he was right. Izzy hadn't said anything about me not sounding like myself. I sat back down on the bed.

"That's my favorite mug," I said.

"So you have a room just like this?" he said. "Dresser from a lawn sale?" I nodded. "Poster of Yosemite Sam? Clock radio?"

I nodded. The clock said 5:30. That reminded me. "I have to go," I said. "My piano lesson is over. Mom will wonder where I am."

The more I talked to Freddie, the more I believed this was really happening, and that I'd have to go home. I also still kind of thought it was a dream. I don't know how you can hold both ideas at once—real and not real—but I did.

"I don't take piano anymore," he said. "I tried it for a while, but I didn't like it, so Mom said I could quit."

Gee, I thought. Why couldn't my mom let me quit? Come to think of it, why couldn't she worry less and laugh more? Why couldn't she be more like this mom?

I bent down to hug Casey again. I didn't want to leave him. But if this was really another world, and not a dream, then maybe—maybe—just maybe I'd see him again. I sure hoped so.

Freddie was thinking the same thing. "You'll come back, won't you?" he said.

"Could I?"

"Yeah! Please! Anytime, man!"

What a friendly guy he was. Probably friendlier than me.

"Okay then!" I said.

He gave me a green hoodie to wear, and I hooded up in case anyone saw me. We snuck downstairs, him leading the way. When we got to the bottom of the stairs, he motioned me past him into the front hall.

"Bye, Mom!" he called into the kitchen. "I'm taking Casey outside to poop."

My mom didn't usually laugh at stuff like this, but Freddie's did.

I ducked out the front door holding Casey's leash. Freddie ran after me, calling for me to slow down. Took him a block to catch up. I hadn't realized I was walking so fast. I crossed the street, like I always do. Freddie asked where I was going.

"The vacant lot is on this side," he said.

"I know, but Lisa Wu's house is on that side too."

"Lisa from Chicago?" said Freddie. "Moved last year? The strong one?"

"Yeah."

"She's nice, eh? Did she invite everyone at your lunch table over to her place on her first day at school?"

"No," I said.

"There was cake and everything. She gave me a corner piece, because I live nearby. Have you ever been to her place?"

"No," I said again.

Lisa did come to our lunch table, all right, and promised to beat up anyone walking on her sidewalk. *I know you live down the street*, she told me with a glare. Then she picked up a corner of the table and let it crash to the floor, spilling my sandwich.

"She hates me," I said.

Freddie looked confused at this. Seemed that his Lisa was nicer than mine. Funny, her house had the same missing bit from the chimney.

We found the open drain without any trouble. "So this is the place," he said. "And there's one just like this in your world?"

"Yeah. Right here too, at the side of the park."

The sun was behind the apartment buildings. I shivered when I took off Freddie's hoodie. Casey stood beside me. I got down on my knees and gave him a big hug. My dog. He licked my face. My dog. I told him I'd see him tomorrow.

"If that's okay with you?" I asked Freddie.

"You bet! Didn't I say so? Come anytime!" He grinned.

A silver airplane sailed across the sky.

"Okay then," I said to Freddie.

"Okay then."

I started down the ladder. Out of the corner of my eye, I could see the airplane bank to turn, and I saw that its wings were curved and pointed, that it seemed to have four legs and a long tail. Then it was out of sight. Weird, I thought, just before I stepped off the bottom rung of the ladder. Next thing I knew I was in total darkness, with nothing under my feet.

Going somewhere for the first time, say your aunt's new apartment across town, takes forever, because you've never been before and you don't recognize anything. But going back is faster. And that's how it was for me, falling back home. It hardly seemed to take any time at all before I landed, bump, at the bottom of the drain, with Casey's ball beside me.

I scrambled to my feet and climbed back up the ladder. It was raining. My backpack and hockey stick were beside the drain. I levered the grate most of the way back, leaving it open so I wouldn't need the stick next time.

There was so much to think about. Casey, alive and well. A brand-new world with another me in it. Casey.

I ran home, tossed my hockey stick back under the porch and paused a minute to catch my breath before opening the front door.

"There you are, Fred! Finally!" Mom leaned against the kitchen counter with a wooden spoon and an expression of relief. "It's almost six; I was getting worried about you. Did you take the long way home from Miss Lea's?"

"Uh, yes," I said.

4

I didn't tell my mom about the other world. You don't, do you? You don't tell your folks about weird cool things that happen to you. First, because maybe you *should* have been doing something else, like going to your piano lesson. And then, because if you tell them, they won't understand, and they'll ask questions you can't answer, and they probably won't let you do it again.

Also, Freddie hadn't told his mom about me, had he? You just don't do it.

"Fred, you're soaked," Mom said to me. "Look at your pants; they're wet up to the knee. And your hands are filthy. Are you sure you're okay?"

I remembered what Freddie had said. "You bet," I said. "But thanks for asking."

She stared at me. "Well, dinner is almost ready, honey. Why don't you change and then come and set the table?"

"Sure, Mom." I ran upstairs.

Izzy was in the bathroom, drying her face. She knew right away that something was different about me.

"What happened?" she asked.

"Nothing."

"Come on, you were smiling. What's going on? What did you do?"

"Nothing," I said.

"See, there it is again. What happened to you, Fred?"

She patted her cheek, staring at herself in the mirror.

I was not going to tell her about upside-down world either. She might pass it on to Mom. And she for sure wouldn't believe me. I did not want to hear her go on and on about her crazy little brother.

"None of your business."

I laid out knives and forks and napkins and glasses.

"What's that you're humming, Fred?"

"Huh?" I didn't know I was humming anything.

"Sounds like you're feeling, well, better," Mom said.

I was going to say, better than what? But I knew what she meant.

"You know, I do feel better."

"Really? Do you mean it?"

"Yeah."

"I knew it," said Izzy. "Something happened to him."

"No it didn't," I insisted.

Mom put her head on one side to look at me. Her mouth puckered up. I thought she was going to cry, but she didn't.

"I—I—that's good," she said. "I'm glad you're feeling better, Fred."

We all sat down to dinner.

Homework done, I carried my dirty clothes down to the basement. That's when I noticed the dog hairs on my jeans. Short, dark hairs all over the wet denim. Casey's hairs.

Breath came out of me in a sudden rush. *Whuff.* The hairs were more than a reminder. They were proof. I wasn't crazy. I wasn't making the whole thing up. The upside-down world was real.

Whuff, indeed.

Lisa Wu caught up to me on my way to school the next day and walked the last block with me. She asked what I was thinking about. I shook my head.

"Is it me, Mouse? You think I'm nice-looking?"

"Uh . . ."

"Do you? The boys in Oak Park were always telling me how nice I looked."

"Uh . . . huh."

"You could come right up and say it, you know, Mouse. Come right up to me and say, 'Lisa, you're nice-looking.' Don't worry, I won't beat you up, even though you're so quiet and small."

In gym that day we had mat work. Log rolls, cartwheels, somersaults. Velma did a bunch of cartwheels in a row and bounced up, hair flying. Would we really be science partners? I went over to tell her how good she was, but she turned away and started talking to Debbie before I got any words out.

I stood on my head. Took me three tries, but I got up. My legs wobbled.

I wanted to try looking down at the ceiling. To get used to it so I wouldn't feel sick when I went to see Casey next time.

"Way to go, Fred!" said the teacher. When she turned away, Lisa pushed me over. I lay on the mat, feeling the blood in my face.

I counted seconds all through the last period, staring out the window at the clouds. When the bell rang, I ran to Izzy's locker to tell her I wouldn't be walking with her. I thought she'd want to know why, but she just nodded.

"I'll be home for dinner," I said.

Harry the Horse came up, and she got all blushy. He was in eighth grade, like Izzy. He wasn't really a horse, but he had a long face and a neighing kind of laugh. *Heaw-heaw-heaw-heaw.* Her phone always had a picture of him on the screen.

"Beat it," she said to me.

There was no one in sight when I got to the vacant lot. The grate was slightly open, the way I had left it. I slid it out of the way and climbed down. I didn't fall right away. I jumped up and down, but nothing happened. I didn't panic. I wasn't crazy. I wasn't! I was standing at the bottom of a sewer drain trying to fall through the universe—but I wasn't crazy!

All right, maybe I was panicking a bit.

I remembered the dog hairs on my pants last night. They were real. I thought of Casey. Which reminded me of his old tennis ball. Which was how the whole adventure started.

The tennis ball was in my pocket. Was it—could it be—the key? I pulled out the ball and held it in my open hand.

Ready . . . set . . .

I took a deep breath and let the ball go.

It was a cloudy day in my world, but the square of sky I could see from the bottom of the drain when I landed was the color of a new swimming pool. I put the ball back in my pocket and grabbed hold of the ladder.

For a half-second, as I was climbing, I felt like I was going down instead of up. My stomach did a 180. But I was getting used to being upside down. This time the sick feeling only lasted a few seconds, and by the time I was standing on the grass beside the drinking fountain, I was totally fine.

Freddie wasn't there yet. I didn't want to go home by myself, in case Izzy was there. I mean Freddie's home — the upside-down home. With upside-down Izzy. Or maybe Mom would be back from work early.

I heard a helicopter and looked up. Yup, there it was, hanging in the air like an insect or a dragon. That reminded me—what had Freddie meant, asking if there were dragons in my world. A real random comment. I thought he was talking about a sports team. Toronto Dragons—who'd probably finish last, whatever league they played in.

I was smiling, I realized. Thinking about Casey. I felt better than fine. I had more energy than I knew what to do with. I jumped as high as I could—*way* higher than normal. Something about being upside down made the gravity different. I felt light, like I could practically fly. I did a handstand and held it for five seconds. I threw myself in the air backward. Seemed like I floated in slow motion, my feet over my head. The world spun around and I landed back on the ground. I'd done a total backflip. I felt featherlight, as if the air itself was helping to hold me up.

"Hey!" said Lisa Wu. "Hey, Freddie!"

I stopped what I was doing.

"How'd you get here?" she asked. She had freckles across the bridge of her nose. Tiny dark dots like pinpricks. I'd never noticed them before. And yet if Freddie and I looked exactly the same, then my Lisa had freckles too. "I saw you in school just now. You were in the hall. How'd you get here so fast?"

I shrugged.

"That was cool, the way you did that flip," she said.

"Uh, thanks."

"Do it again."

"Uh."

"Do it."

I took a step back. "Are you going to beat me up if I don't?"

She looked puzzled for a moment. Then she laughed. "Beat you up? Why would I beat you up? You're such a joker, Freddie."

She punched me on the arm. "Such a joker!" she said.

Her punch hurt. Maybe she wasn't mean in this world, but she was still strong.

"So would you do the flip again?" she said. "Please?"

So strange to hear the word *please* in her mouth. She looked almost nice, saying it. So I did another flip.

"Cool," she said, and walked away.

A minute later Freddie came running up, calling hey, hey. He was smiling too. He asked me how I was doing and told me he was fine, fine, fine.

"I saw Lisa talking to you," he said.

"She wondered how you got here so fast," I said.

"I saw her heading toward you, so I hid behind the fence until she went. I was thinking, what if she saw us both together? Funny, eh! We'll have to think of a story for if people do catch us. Maybe we could be brothers, huh? Twins! Hey, how did you learn to do that back-flip? You are super talented. You looked like someone on TV! Can you show me how to do it? I'd love to learn. Come to think of it, we couldn't be brothers, because people know I don't have a brother. How about cousins? We could be identical cousins. Hey, I like that shirt. Where'd you get it? Mom buys most of my stuff. I could tell her to look for something like that."

He ran out of breath at last. Freddie talked more than I did and didn't worry as much. Identical cousins? That story wouldn't fool his mom or sister. And they were way more likely to be a problem than any stranger.

"Let's go see Casey," I said.

"Okay then!" So funny to hear him say that.

I followed him to the house. Casey met us at the back door. My heart got louder the moment I saw him. My knees wobbled with happiness. I leaned over to put my arms around him and let him lick my face.

Mom was out until dinner. We decided to take Casey for a walk. I gave Freddie my shirt from yesterday—carried it in my knapsack all day.

"Izzy saw me wearing this," I said. "You keep it."

"You mean *my* sister Izzy," he said.

I nodded.

"Because you have a sister Izzy too, right? And that's what you call her? So when you say Izzy saw you, you're talking about my sister Izzy, not your sister Izzy."

My head was starting to hurt.

"Keep the shirt," I said.

High Park is only a few blocks from the house and it's the biggest park in the city. There are playgrounds and tennis courts, a restaurant and a farm, hills and rivers, and a huge pond, where you can skate in the winter. There are squirrels, raccoons and joggers. And a million trees and bushes and paths. I used to take Casey there all the time.

We went up to Dog Heaven, an open grassy place near the top end of the park, where dogs can go off leash. Freddie and I both had tennis balls, and Casey chased after them for a while. Then he started chasing after a beagle named Lady Godiva. Lady Godiva's owner was an old woman with a handbag. I'd never seen her, but she knew Freddie and came over to say hi. Freddie introduced me as his cousin, and the woman said it was nice to meet me.

"You two look a lot alike," she said.

"Everyone says so," Freddie agreed. "Maybe he's a little taller. What do you think? Is he? Is he a little taller?"

I stood up straight.

"Maybe," said the woman.

"But I'm more outgoing," said Freddie. "It comes from living in the city. My cousin here is from a long way away, so far it seems like the other side of the world. He's shy."

The woman smiled and took Lady Godiva home.

I punched Freddie. He punched me back. *Shy?* I said. *Shy?* He started to laugh, and I joined him. Then we noticed Casey a few feet away from us, stretched out so that his back was completely flat. One paw was raised. He was staring fixedly into the middle distance.

"Look at that!" said Freddie. "It's like he's a what-do-you-call-it—a pointer. I didn't know he could do that. He's never done it before. Did he do that for you? Did he? And what kind of animal is he pointing at, anyway?"

A blobby thing, about the size and shape of a soccer ball, mostly white.

"Too big for a squirrel. And it's lighter—almost white. Is it—oh, look at the ears! See, Fred?"

I saw. The animal had put its ears up, and now—even from where we were—it was easy to tell what it was.

"It's a rabbit! You don't see too many of those here. And look at Casey go!"

We ran after the dog, calling him to come back. The rabbit bolted. Man it moved fast! I saw its puff-ball tail bouncing up and down, and then it vanished into the underbrush. Casey was right after it, barking wildly.

I ran as fast as I could, which turned out to be faster than I ever had before. Not running—more like leaping. Every stride was carrying me yards and yards. I felt like I was running on the moon, moving so far with each stride that I had trouble balancing. After an extra-long leap, I fell forward and had to put my arms out to save myself.

"Hey!" Freddie called from way behind. "How are you doing that?"

I reached the trees. I could hear the dog ahead of me, crashing through the underbrush. "Casey, stay!" I yelled.

I had to slow down. I was afraid that if I moved too fast I'd bump into a tree and knock myself out. I followed the sound of Casey's steady barking.

I finally caught up to him at the base of a giant oak. It had to be one of the tallest in the whole park. The trunk was wider than my two arms stretched out—if it were hollow you could drive through it. The tree stood in the middle of a clearing, the ribbed bark furry with old moss. The branches, far overhead, stuck out at random right angles. Twisted roots as thick as my waist stuck up from the ground and seethed round the base of the tree, like waves around a rock.

Casey was barking, barking like crazy. But not at the rabbit.

5

The thing knelt by the base of the tree. Long snout and snaky body, clawed feet, leathery wings, greenish silvery scales. It was bigger than a horse. When it breathed, jets of steam came out its snout, covering it from head to foot. The steam blew away, and there it was again.

A dragon.

It tried to fly away. Its wings flapped heavily as it heaved its bulk off the ground and then fell back.

I was so amazed, I couldn't move or speak. Couldn't think. It was like meeting the what's-their-names in the Greek myths, the ones who turn you to stone. You know who I mean. Them.

Everything was still for a second. It was like we were in a picture—a boy, a dog, a dragon. I trembled. Casey growled. The dragon steamed. The wind came up, rustling grass and leaves the way it did at home on any old September afternoon.

I heard crashing off to my left. Freddie's voice (which

still didn't sound like mine) got louder as he came closer. That broke the spell. I grabbed Casey's collar.

"Come on!" I said, trying to pull him away from the dragon. That's when I noticed that one of the dragon's forefeet—claws, whatever—was caught in the tangle of tree roots. That's how come it couldn't fly. Its long skinny snout rippled and ruffled—like its lip was quivering and it was about to cry.

Did I feel sympathy? Nope. It was a dragon! Did I feel sympathy for a hornet trapped in a storm window?

I pulled Casey away as Freddie charged into the clearing.

"Hey, there you are! You are fast, man! Where did you learn to run like—"

He stopped dead beside me. His chest rose and fell as he panted.

"Oh," he said. His face went blank. His shoulders drooped as he let out a long breath.

"Okay then," he said.

He wasn't amazed at all. I guess he was used to dragons.

I tried to pull him and Casey back. We had to get out of here before the thing started breathing fire all over us! But Freddie shook off my hand and approached the dragon.

"Hey there, little girl," he said. "You look like you're in trouble. Let's see if I can help."

"Don't, Freddie!" I shouted.

"Nothing we can do about it," he said without looking back. "If it's my time and she's come for me, there's nothing I can do. I'm ready."

"What?"

He bent beside the dragon.

What now? I wasn't going to leave Freddie, but if this dragon was the kind in stories or video games, it could start breathing fire at any time.

I watched closely from behind a tree, ready to grab Freddie if I could help him. Ready to grab Casey and run if I couldn't.

Freddie was still talking. "There, there," I heard him say as he twisted the trapped claw around and pulled it free. It looked smaller than the other claws and sort of curled up. A slight deformity. The dragon would be able to fly okay but would have trouble walking or landing.

"There you go, girl. I'm going to call you Stumbler."

He backed away slowly, making no attempt to run, flexing his right hand open and shut. I watched past his shoulder. Her eyes—I'd never thought of dragons as girls before—were intensely blue. She lifted her freed claw and put it down again, testing it, but the gesture looked like a wave.

Freddie waved back. And turned away.

"Let's go," he said. "I guess it's not time."

"So there are no dragons in your world? None at all?"

Freddie slurped his milk shake.

"In stories," I said. "And video games. But they're not real."

We were at the restaurant in the middle of High Park, slurping away—me and Freddie on milk shakes, Casey at our feet from a metal water bowl. We had fries too.

"So how do people know when it's their time?" he asked.

"What?"

"If there are no dragons to carry them off, how do they disappear? How do they get to the mountain?"

"What are you talking about?"

"The mountain—Dragon Mountain. You know, the one way north of the city? How do people get there without dragons to carry them?"

I shook my head without saying anything. He was using words I knew, but what he was saying didn't make any sense to me.

"Or animals—or anything. What about Casey?" he said. "Your Casey, I mean."

The dog looked up from his water, and Freddie patted him.

"You said he was gone. Did you see the dragon carry him off?"

"No," I said. "I came downstairs and he was dead."

"His body was there?"

"Yeah. The body was there, but he was dead. Gone? You know?"

Now it was Freddie's turn to look totally blank. Neither of us understood what the other was talking about.

I held onto Casey's leash on the way back to Wright Avenue. Remembering his little body lying on the kitchen floor back home made me feel terrible all over again. What an awful morning that had been.

"I have to go home," I said. "Or Mom will worry."

I stopped.

"Would she worry if you were late?"

Freddie laughed at that. "Mom doesn't worry about much. I mean, she cares. When we're sick, she takes us to the doctor, makes sure we take our pills. But if I was late, she'd shrug and expect me when I got there. She's not a worrier, you know?"

I shook my head. "No," I said. "I don't know at all."

Freddie smiled.

"So you coming back tomorrow?"

That became our routine for the next few days. Freddie would meet me on his walk with Casey and we'd hang out until dinnertime. We went along Queen Street and down Roncesvalles and across the Gardiner Expressway to the lake, and places like that. Upside-down Toronto looked exactly the same as the one I knew. It was fun. Freddie did most of the talking, but I made him laugh a few times. We didn't talk about dragons again. They were strange, all right—but the whole world was strange. Casey being alive was what mattered to me. I focused on that.

Freddie always walked me to the drain—the portal, he called it. He stared down into the sewer. His face, and Casey's, were the last things I saw before I dropped. Once I asked him if he wanted to come back to my world with me.

"Why?" he said.

"To see it," I said. "You'd probably think everything was upside down."

"I don't know," he said. "It sounds weird. It's different for you, Fred. You come here to see Casey 'cause you miss him. But I don't miss him."

"What *do* you miss? Anything?"

It was another bright afternoon. The sun flashed off a car going by on Wabash Avenue.

He shrugged. "Maybe I miss something but don't know it."

"If you missed it, you'd know."

I was careful going back and forth between worlds. Fortunately the drain was in an isolated part of Sorauren

Park, so no one ever saw me climbing in or out. And I made sure to change clothes and wash my hands when I got home, so Mom never found out.

She noticed something about me though. "You're smiling again, Fred," she said, maybe a week later, at dinner. "You've been smiling a lot lately, haven't you."

"Maybe," I said.

"What do you think, Izzy? Isn't your brother smiling more?"

My sister shrugged.

"I'm finished," she said. "I'm going to Harry's house, okay?"

So Mom and I were alone with dessert. She reached across the table to pat the back of my hand.

"I'm glad you're feeling better these days, honey," she said. "You've been so quiet. So low. Ever since . . ."

She didn't want to say it.

"Ever since Casey," I said.

She opened her mouth and then closed it, like she was surprised by my answer. I smiled at her around a bit of ice cream. How surprised would she be if I told her that I'd taken Casey to High Park two hours ago? He'd chased this one gray squirrel around and around an oak tree, continuing to circle the tree as the squirrel climbed. When the rodent was out of sight, Casey took two dizzy steps and fell over. Freddie and I had to hang onto ourselves we were laughing so hard.

Mom took a bite of apple pie.

"I didn't want to be sad," I said. "But I couldn't help it."

"Oh, honey, I know. I get sad too," she said.

"Yeah, I guess you do."

I might not have noticed this if it wasn't that Freddie's mom seemed so much happier than mine. Was my mom that happy before Casey died?

"I try to hide it," she said. "I don't want to be crying in front of you kids. And there's the office too. Mrs. Loewen depends on me."

Mom works for an insurance company, doing something with claims. That means she gives people money when they get run over by cars or fall off ladders. Mrs. Loewen's her boss. Mom didn't always work. I remember her being home when I went to junior school. But she works now. She says she likes it.

"Dr. Nussbaum will be pleased when he sees you tomorrow," she said. "You've come a long way in a couple of weeks."

"Do I have to keep seeing the doctor?" I asked. "If I'm feeling better and all."

"Let's let him decide that, okay, honey?"

She smiled. Not a chuckle. A hopeful kind of lip-lift. If only she could have as much fun as Freddie's mom, then maybe I'd have as much fun as Freddie.

That thought made me feel disloyal.

"This is good pie," I said. "Really good. Thanks, Mom."

"Bought it myself," she said.

6

Dear Freddie,
Can't meet you today. Sorry. Doctor's appointment.
Hug Casey for me. See you guys tomorrow.
  Fred.
PS—We have to work out a message system.

I wrote this when I woke up. I planned to give it to
Freddie at lunch, so he wasn't hanging around the
drain waiting and waiting for me after school. But
when the bell rang, I couldn't find the note. I searched
my whole binder, but it wasn't there. I quickly scribbled
another one, stuck it in my pocket with the tennis ball
and headed for the vacant lot.

I was used to the up-down thing. Hardly felt sick at
all. I was getting the hang of the lighter gravity too. I just
zoomed to school and stood outside the fence, trying to
spot Freddie in the crowd of kids hanging out after lunch.

There was a basketball game going on. Blue shirts
and white shirts. Miss Stapleton, the gym teacher, was

refereeing. The players on the white team were from 6D, my class and Freddie's. Blue team was 6A. Freddie had the ball. He tried a pass to Mike, but Lance Levy intercepted it, raced down to the other basket and scored an easy layup. When the ball went through the net, he pumped his fist.

"Hey!" I called through the fence. "Hey, kid!"

He was by himself. He usually was. His name was Purvis Stackpole. I pretended not to know his name. "Come here, kid," I called.

He came over to the fence.

"Do you know Freddie Berdit?" I asked.

Purvis sniffed up a long one. He did that a lot. One of the reasons why he was usually alone.

"Yeah, yeah, I know Freddie," he said. "He's my friend. He makes me laugh."

"Give this to Freddie and say it's from his cousin."

Purvis squinted at me. His glasses were twisted.

"Who's Freddie's cousin?"

I'd gone too fast for him. "I am," I said.

"You're Freddie's cousin?"

"Yup."

He nodded a bunch of times. "Cousin, huh? Yeah. You look like him. Are you funny too?"

"No."

That made him laugh. "Yes you are!" he said. "Yes you are! You are funny!"

He stared at the note in his hand.

"This says *Freddie* on it," he said.

"Yes. It's for him. He's playing basketball over there. See?"

Purvis nodded, sniffed again and headed across the playground holding my note.

Lance was at the foul line. He sank two shots, pumping his fist after each one.

The bell rang.

I ran, back to the vacant lot, down and back up again, reaching my own school with no time left, joining the end of the line just as it snaked its way through the double doors. I was puffing like a whale after running the three blocks up Sorauren and along Westminster. Things were heavier in the right-side-up world. I moved slower, weighed more, worked harder.

All the way back I thought about Purvis. I had hardly said two words to him all year. Freddie was a nicer guy than I was.

Mom and I took the subway downtown. It's my favorite way to travel. You hear the train in the distance, squealing. Then you feel a rush of hot wind. You see a light in the distance, getting bigger, and hear a rushing sound as the train hurtles at you. The future is coming. Scary and cool.

"Stand back, Fred!"

Mom grabbed me as the train pulled in. I shook free.

"Okay," I said. "Okay."

Dr. Nussbaum's waiting room was painted bright yellow, with posters of Flynn Goster and other cartoon heroes on the wall. There were toys and picture books and stuffed animals. I picked up a Phlegm comic. Mom sat beside me and stared straight ahead of her. Something was wrong, and I didn't know what. She wore the smile that meant she wanted to scream. I hadn't seen that one in a while.

The inner door opened and a teenager came out shaking his head. Mom told me to wait and went into the inner office to talk to the doctor without me.

The teenager stared at me. "What are you laughing at?" he said. "You crazy? Is that why you're laughing?"

I didn't say anything. I wasn't laughing.

"I've been reading about crazy people. I know how their minds work. Do you have frogs living in the bottom of your toilet tank?"

"No."

"You sure?"

I blinked. "Pretty sure."

"Do you worry about meteors falling onto your house?"

"No."

"Do you believe that microscopic bugs eat your skin off of you every night—all of it, even between the toes—and a new skin grows in its place?"

"Ew," I said.

"Yeah. Ew is right."

He was smiling now. I smiled back.

"Maybe you're not crazy, after all," he said. "Do you want a mint?"

He took a packet from his pocket, squeezed one out for me and then left.

Dr. Nussbaum's office was set up like a playroom, with all sorts of games on the shelves and floor. When I first came to see him, we played with dolls the whole hour long. He had a whole family of dolls—a mommy and a daddy, a boy and a girl, a baby, and a dog and a cat. He'd asked me to make up a story about the family. The dolls were real-looking, with browny-black hair and soft skin, wearing clothes and shoes that did up with Velcro. The dog was dark, like Casey.

No dolls today. We sat on comfy chairs and talked. Mine was oatmeal colored. He took his usual worn brown leather desk chair, with wheels.

"Your mom says you're starting to smile a little bit more than you were," said the doctor. "Maybe have a little more fun. You think so too?"

I nodded.

"Do you still think about your dog very much?"

Dr. Nussbaum was a big sweater guy. I mean he wore big sweaters. Today's had triangles on it. He pushed up the sleeves and leaned back in his leather chair.

"You want me to say no, don't you?"

"Nope," he said. "I want you to tell the truth. It's normal to miss your dog when he dies. Hey, I had a dog named Kerry when I was a boy. A Weimaraner—gray, with floppy ears. I used to rollerblade with her all the way down to the Beaches and back. When she was hit by a car, I cried for days. I don't cry anymore, but I still miss her, thirty years later."

He smiled, lips only, no teeth.

"It's okay to miss Casey. You don't have to be brave to please your mom. Or me. Or anyone. Okay?"

"Okay," I said.

"So are you really feeling happier, Fred? It seems so to me, looking at you now. There is a sparkle in your eye. Your mom says she heard you singing a TV commercial around the house a couple of days ago. Is that right?"

I nodded.

"That's great. Real progress. But I guess you don't like your piano lessons, eh?"

"I don't?"

"Your mom says you've skipped your last few lessons. Your teacher called to ask where you were."

I shut my mouth. Mom never mentioned it.

"And then there's this note."

He leaned forward. Held out a familiar piece of paper. "Your mom found it in your room. Seems like you wrote it to someone named Freddie. You want him to hug Casey for you. Who's Freddie?"

He waited. I didn't say anything.

"Freddie's your name. A version of your name. What can you tell me about Freddie?"

I didn't know what to say.

"Well, how about this. Do you like Freddie?"

"Sure," I said, without thinking.

"Good. So he's a person, Freddie. Someone you talk to."

This was a minefield. I was afraid to take a step.

"Uh," I said.

Dr. Nussbaum has a way of making his voice soft and yet piercing at the same time. Like a golf commentator. He spun around in his chair, leaned toward me and put his hands on his knees.

"Tell me more about Freddie," he said. "Is Freddie *you*?"

I didn't know what to say. I mean, I really didn't know.

7

"Oh my gosh!" said Freddie, when I told him the next day. "Oh, that is amazing! And hilarious. And awful. What did you say to this doc?"

Freddie's family doctor was Dr. Davila, like mine, but he didn't go to Dr. Nussbaum.

"What could I tell him? The truth? 'Freddie is a parallel version of myself living in an upside-down world, where my dead dog is alive.'"

Freddie laughed. "Maybe not."

"I said I wrote the note because I was sad, and that Freddie was someone to talk to, like an imaginary friend. He said that writing down thoughts and feelings was a good idea, and was there anyone else I wanted to write to? He asked if I ever felt like I was outside my body, watching myself do stuff. I said no. I said that I really was feeling happier. Then we talked about Casey some more. Then it was time to go."

"You know, I think that's the most you've ever said at once, Fred."

He spoke through a mouthful of Cap'n Crunch. We were in his bedroom. He was on the bed. I lay on the floor with my head on Casey's back and my empty bowl beside me.

"Well, you're easy to talk to."

"Like an imaginary friend?"

"No, like the real thing."

We smiled at each other.

"What about the piano lessons?" he asked.

"Mom asked if I liked playing piano, and I said not really. So she said I didn't have to go anymore."

"Okay then! Fantastic. It's a winner!"

"Maybe," I said.

"For sure!"

Maybe it was a winner. No more scales or claw hands. But it's never fun when your mom's upset. It was a real quiet trip home. All evening long she'd watched me out of the corner of her eye.

Freddie's mom and sister were downtown, shopping. That's how I thought of them—*his* family. I liked his mom, what I heard from her. I wished my mom could be more like her—more fun loving, happier—but I never thought of her as mine. Same with his Izzy, who spent a lot of time with the boyfriend she called Handsome Harry. She was my friend's big sister, not mine.

Casey was different. He was both of ours. We shared him.

Anyway, it was afternoon, and we had the house to ourselves. The place looked almost the same as mine, but not quite. This bathroom tap dripped, like ours did, but the stopper for the sink was still attached to the metal chain and ours had fallen off. Izzy's room here had busy wallpaper too, the right color but a different pattern. Freddie's mom had twice as much stuff as mine—there were clothes all over.

Freddie had the same video games I did. We played *Badge of Glory* and *Zombie Killz* and *NBA Tonite*. Our skill levels matched exactly, like our height and arm length. Same number of kills, same number of shots, same score every time. When we played on the same side, we totally kicked our opponents. The zombies went down like grass under the mower. Our last NBA game—Raptors versus Lakers—was 140–40 for us.

"I love basketball," he said. "I just wish I was better at it in real life."

"I saw you on the intramural team at lunch."

"Oh yeah? We're lousy, eh? Did you see much of the game? We were playing 6A. They killed us. Lance must have scored twenty points."

"Lance Levy," I said.

"Yeah. The human fist pump. Was he in your class last year? You know he would celebrate when he spelled a word right." Freddie cleared his throat. "*Perspective.*

P-E-R-S-P-E-C-T-I-V-E." He said this in a kind of whine, like Lance talked. "And Mrs. Bjork would nod and Lance would go, *Yesss*! And pump his fist."

I laughed. Freddie was a funny guy, just like poor Purvis said.

"I like basketball too," I said. "I didn't go out for our class team, though."

"Why not?"

"I don't know. I didn't feel like it."

"Do you want to play now?"

"Uh . . ."

"Come on!"

It took me a while to get used to the game here, for an absolutely *awesome* reason. The ball and court were the same, but I wasn't. I was way better. I went up for my first layup and found myself staring at the rim. That's right—the rim of the basket was at eye level. I hadn't even jumped hard and I was ten feet in the air. I was so surprised that I threw the ball right over the backboard.

Freddie stood back at the foul line, his mouth open.

"Can you do that again?" he said.

"I'll try."

So I did. He threw me a pass, and I took it and went up and up. I tried to stuff the ball, but missed, and ended up clinging to the rim with both hands.

"I love it!" he said. "Do it again, Fred! Come on. I'll feed you the ball."

Third time I concentrated on the basket getting closer and closer as I floated up. I brought my hands over my head and dropped the ball through the hoop easy as whistling.

Freddie applauded.

"You're amazing!" he said. "How do you do that? It was like at the park the other day, going after Casey. I was running as fast as I could, but you were, like, already a football field ahead. *Zoom! Zowie!* You're some kind of superstar, Fred. You should be playing for your class team! You should be playing for the city!"

I had to smile at his enthusiasm.

"Things are different here," I said.

The sun went behind a cloud. Casey was barking at a nearby seagull, straining at his leash, which we'd tied to a garbage can. Time for me to go.

"I won't be around after school tomorrow," he said. "Velma and I are working on our water cycle project. We'll be at her house. Maybe the next day, or the one after that?"

"I don't know. I have to see Dr. Nussbaum again this week," I said.

"Well, let me know when you can come. I'll check the shed."

We had decided to use Freddie's backyard shed as

our post office. There was a shelf where we could leave notes.

Shadows were lengthening across Sorauren Park. I was sitting with my legs dangling down the open drain, tickling Casey behind his ears.

"Quick, someone's coming!"

I hugged the dog and dropped into the dark.

While I fell, I wondered if Freddie liked Velma as much as I did. An afternoon at her place? Not bad, I thought. Not bad at all.

I saw Dr. Nussbaum again on Friday. And twice more the week after that. He thought we were getting close to something. He gave me a mirror. The kind you hold in your hand. He wanted me to look in the mirror and tell what I saw. Weird, huh? He asked again if there was someone I wanted to write to. I shook my head. *You sure?* he said. He wondered if there might be something I was holding back.

I couldn't—just couldn't—tell him the truth. How would it sound? *I fell through a hole in the earth.* Crazy is how it would sound. Frogs in the toilet tank.

Speaking of that, I saw that kid a couple more times. His name was Max. He was a year older than me. His stepfather owned a grocery store. Max had stolen a bunch of sardine cans from the store, opened them and dumped them into the family swimming pool. Now everyone was mad at him.

I smiled when he told me this. It was a funny picture, a pool full of sardines.

I asked the doctor when I would be cured. He said that it wasn't a question of me being sick. But there was something blocking me, and I couldn't move on until I'd got past it. "It's as if a dead tree has fallen across the road," he said. "You've got to get around it before you can continue your journey."

"Is Casey the tree?" I asked.

He smiled.

"Casey's dead," I said.

He nodded. "Go on," he said.

But I couldn't.

8

Freddie spread a giant sheet of brown paper across the bedroom floor, taped it down and got out a big box of crayons from his desk drawer. He'd already drawn outlines of the picture. There was a sun, river, ocean, cloud, house.

"Now, get going, Fred," he said. "We have to fill this in by next week."

The house he'd sketched had lots of detail. He was a good artist. I'd never cared that much about what things looked like. "There's someone taking a bath here," I said.

"Sure!" he smiled. "That's part of the water cycle. Velma is doing an experiment in front of the class to show the water cycle, and I'm doing this picture to explain it."

"Do you like Velma?" I asked.

"Not that much. She's mean. She called Mike a minority."

"Do you jump inside when she looks at you?"

"Huh?"

"Is it like an electric shock? A kind of *zing* feeling?"

He handed me a light blue crayon. "Get coloring," he said.

Freddie explained the water cycle to me. He did a good job—better than Miss Pullteeth when our class got to it the next week.

"When you take a bath, you drain the water, right?" he said. "And it runs down the waste pipe to the sewer and then to the lake. And the sun heats it and it evaporates into the sky. And then next time it rains the water comes down to earth again. The city collects rainwater in a reservoir and pipes it through to your house. So that when you have another bath, you're using the same water as before."

He showed me the things on his drawing—reservoir, water pipe, clouds.

"What's this?" I pointed at an animal way under the ground below the house. "Is it a dragon?"

I hadn't seen any since that one in the park, but I kept checking for them. Wondering about them.

"That's a dinosaur," said Freddie. "Do you have those in your world? Like dragons, millions of years ago. No wings on that one—it's a stegosaurus. I put it in because water has been going around and around and around the world forever."

"Always the same water?"

"Absolutely. It rained on the dinosaurs and evaporated

into the clouds, and rained on the ancient Egyptians and evaporated again, and rained on the Iroquois and the pioneers and your grandparents and you. It's all the same water. It never goes away. It's never used up. That's the water cycle."

It took a minute for the idea of something lasting forever, not ever disappearing, to sink into my brain.

"My favorite part of the project is the experiment," he said. "We're going to take sweat from the class and show how it's part of the water cycle."

"Hey, that's smart. Did Velma think of that?"

"No, it's my idea. I haven't told her yet."

I thought of Velma with her hand on my arm, collecting my sweat. Or on my cheek. *Zing.*

The paper stretched from the bed to the window. Freddie was on his hands and knees, filling in the house details. I started near the other end, coloring a mountain. We had the same box of crayons, but I didn't look after mine the way he did. All his were in the box, all sharpened. Mine were mostly nubby and quite a few were missing.

I got down on my stomach and worked away with brown crayon until Casey jiggled me.

"Oh no," I said. "I went outside the lines. Sorry, Freddie. Your mountain has a jaggedy brown bump sticking out of it."

He came over.

"No problem," he said. "Watch."

He took my brown crayon and a green one and a black one, and with three or four strokes, he turned my jaggedy bump into a pine tree.

"There. Mountains have trees at the bottom," he said.

"Hey, that's good!" I said. "You're good."

"Thanks."

"How come you can draw and I can't?" I said.

He shrugged. "How come you can jump ten feet in the air and I can't?"

"I can't jump very high back home."

"Well—I guess I'm different from you, then."

"Yeah."

He was too. Back home I couldn't jump or draw. Or play with my dog.

I looked up a few minutes later and found that it wasn't a few minutes later. It was a lot later.

"I have to go!" I said.

Mom would be getting home from work now. She'd ask where I'd been and why I was late, and I'd have to lie. I should have left a half hour ago. Crap. The same water may go on and on forever, but time is now and then it's gone.

I wanted to leave right away, but Izzy was in the hall outside, yelling down to her mom about laundry. I pulled open the bedroom window—it stuck at the bottom, just like mine at home—and peered out.

"What are you doing, Fred?"

"I'm going to jump," I said.

"Can you?"

"I think so. It's not much higher than a basketball net."

I perched for a second on the sill. It looked like a long way down, but the drainpipe was within reach. I wouldn't dare do it from home, but I was running late and feeling the light-headedness of this place. I grabbed hold of the drainpipe and scrambled down. Freddie leaned out the window to wave.

A guy in a hard hat stared at me as I raced—slowly— across my Sorauren Park, pushing Casey's ball back into my pocket and adjusting to the heavy right-side-upness of things.

Turned out that all of us were late for dinner. I got in the door one minute ahead of Izzy and two ahead of Mom. No one asked where I'd been. Mom had picked up a pasta thing on the way home from work and we had that. Tasted gluey.

The dishwasher made sloshing sounds as it filled up. I thought about the water inside, cleaning off our pasta dishes and draining away into the lake, where it would evaporate and then become rain, the same rain that had fallen on my mom when she was a little girl.

9

Didn't matter how awful or disgusting or plain boring something was, Miss Pullteeth would get excited about it. "Way to go, Kleenex!" she would say, when one of us came in with a cold and spent a whole minute blowing our nose. "All right, Team Canada! Way to try!!" she said when they lost a hockey game to the US or the Swedes. Miss Pullteeth wore clothes she'd made herself out of odd bits of fabric—dresses, pants, pullovers. She was tall and thin and the clothes flapped around her body like flags on a pole. She had big hands and she liked to clap them. Today she was clapping for me, because I had volunteered to be South America.

"Way to go, Fred! Come on up here."

I don't know why I did it. Ever since . . . well, for what seemed forever I'd sat in the back of the class with my head down. Hadn't felt like saying anything. We had Friday spelling bees, last one standing won a candy bar, and I always got my word wrong on purpose so I could sit down. But today Miss Pullteeth had held up a bunch of cardboard cutouts and said, "Who wants to be part of the world?" And I found myself with my hand up.

I took the cardboard map of South America and stood up at the front of the class with Paul, Rider, Lisa, Renee, Mike and Tara.

"Hey, look!" Velma whispered to Carmen next to her. "Mike is Asia!"

From his expression, I couldn't tell if he'd heard the comment. Lisa Wu heard. "And I'm North America," she said. "Immigration, eh? Get used to it."

She glared at Velma. She didn't like her any more than Freddie did. Velma sneered back at her. Man, she had a cute sneer.

Miss Pullteeth had us stand together to show how the continents used to fit into each other like a jigsaw puzzle, back at the beginning of the world. Then she had us spread apart. Renee went off by herself at the back to be Australia. Tara and Mike and Paul were in a kind of huddle over by the door, since Africa, Asia and Europe are all together. Lisa and I were holding hands, two continents linked in the middle. She wore dark nail polish.

My first time ever holding hands with a girl who was not my sister. I felt my face getting warmer.

"And then a hundred years ago," said Miss Pullteeth, "they built the Panama Canal, and the link between North and South America was cut."

She nodded to us. "You can let go of each other's hands now," she whispered.

I could feel the pressure of Lisa's fingers even after she dropped my hand.

Lunch recess. Mike Lee was losing to Lance Levy at one-on-one. Lance was fist pumping after every basket, as usual. Finally Mike scored.

"That's it, Asia!" I yelled. "You can do it!"

He stared over at me, startled, then broke into a smile. I held out my hand and he slapped it as he ran past me.

"What's so funny?"

"Huh?"

"Were you laughing at the veal parmigiana?"

"Oh. No, Mom, it's fine. It's good."

I'd been thinking about my races with Freddie that afternoon. Him inside the house, me outside. *One, two, three, go!* he shouted and ran up the stairs to his room. Meanwhile, I was climbing up the outside of the house, using the drainpipe as a ladder. There were metal things sticking out of the brick to attach the drainpipe. I could leap to the first one, pull myself up and then shin up the rest of the drainpipe to Freddie's window. Casey barked and ran around in circles.

Voices, arguing. I looked up from my veal again. Izzy was asking if she could go to her boyfriend's house and watch TV. Mom was saying sure, but she had to be home by nine. Izzy was saying that was too early. Mom was saying tough.

I thought about Harry and his long chin. Handsome Harry to Freddie. Harry the Horse to me. I didn't mean to smile, but I guess I did. Izzy saw me and thought I was making fun of her.

"Shut up, brat," she said to me.

"Isabel!" said my mom.

"You shut up, Izzy!" I said.

Mom opened her mouth and closed it again.

Isabel stood in the doorway with a hurt expression on her face. Hurt? I mean angry. "Aren't you going to yell at Fred for saying shut up? You yelled at me."

"I . . ." said Mom. "I . . . want to yell at both of you!"

"Yeah, sure." Isabel glared at her. And me. And left. So it was just two of us at the table. And one of us was crying.

I wanted to run away, but I couldn't. I cleared my throat and tried a *there, there* to see how it would go.

Mom—this was a surprise—laughed through her tears.

"Your face," she said. "You're so concerned and uncomfortable. Did you think I was upset?"

"Aren't you?"

"No. I'm happy. You yelled at your sister."

"And that made you happy?"

"You sounded like yourself. Your old self. Dr. Nussbaum was right. You're making progress."

She blew her nose.

"Don't get me wrong. I'm still angry at you skipping piano lessons without telling me. Why couldn't you just say? Anyway, that's over for now. You're not hiding anything, and you're angry at Izzy. Things are normal. Oh, you don't understand, Fred. I've been afraid to leave you, even for an evening, let alone overnight. But the way you're acting now, I'm hopeful. It's a big deal, honey. That's why I'm crying. Sorry to make you uncomfortable."

Freddie always seemed happy to hang around his mom. Was that because he was cooler than I was, or because she was cooler than Mom?

"What's for dessert?" I said.

↑o

Wet afternoon. Rain dripped off eaves and trees and made little dents in puddles. My hair hung limp. I brushed it out of my eyes. Freddie left a note for me in his shed.

Mom is making me go to the dentist. Teeth, am I right?
Sorry, Fred. See you tomorrow!

His writing looked just like mine.

Shinning up the drainpipe, I had a moment of panic. What if the house wasn't empty? Mom always made Izzy's and my appointments on the same day and went with us. What if Freddie's mom didn't? What if she was inside right now? What if she caught me? What story could I possibly tell her?

But the house was empty. I squeezed into Freddie's room, and there was Casey. He'd heard me climbing up. He barked and wagged and wriggled and jumped all over me. And I was glad to be there.

"Hey, boy." I hugged him hard and put my nose right up against his fur. He smelled like I remembered him when I first got him. Like my dog, Casey.

I found I was crying.

Weird, eh? I'd been playing with Casey for weeks. Why was I suddenly weepy?

I hadn't cried much when he died. Not even that first night, alone in my quiet room when I'd been used to him breathing beside me. I had stared up into the dark, dry eyed and numb.

Dr. Nussbaum and I talked about this. He told me not to worry. He said I'd cry as much as I had to when I was ready to. So maybe I was ready now, because here I was blowing my nose and then starting again right away, a tap that wouldn't shut off.

Casey didn't mind. He panted and licked my face.

I went downstairs and played chase the ball with him in the living room, and kept crying. When it was time to go, I knelt down to give him a big hug.

A police car was parked in the street outside. It made a bleeping sound to get my attention and the officer got out.

"What were you doing in there, kid?" he called.

I sniffed. "I live there."

"We got a report about someone breaking in," he said. "Kid in a gray sweatshirt and jeans, climbing up the drainpipe."

"Oh, yeah. That was me. I was locked out."

"What's your name?"

"Fred Berdit."

"Your mom or dad around, Fred?" he asked.

"My what?"

"Your parents?"

"Oh, yeah. I mean, no. Not around. Not here. My dad is—I mean my mom's at the dentist with my sister," I said.

My throat felt tight. I don't know if it was the policeman's suspicion or a reaction from the crying. I took rapid breaths to fill my lungs and—and—and took off down the street. I don't know what I was thinking. No. Yeah. No, I had to get away. That's what I was thinking. Had to get away. Had to.

I looked back from Sorauren Avenue. The cop was staring after me like I was a ghost or a superhero. How had I got so far so fast? I turned into the park, found the drain, jumped.

The trip between worlds was time-out. Like sitting on the sidelines, watching your big sister play soccer. Like standing on the subway platform, waiting for the future to arrive.

Falling, I thought about the day I picked Casey out. It was last year about this time. Not summer, but summer was coming. Sunshiny weather, T-shirts and shorts. Mom and I took the streetcar along Queen Street to the other side of the city. We sat at the back, with the sun on our necks and our shadows stretching in front of us on the floor of the streetcar. She was wearing her green jeans again—she seemed to have the same clothes on forever, last summer. She sighed and yawned and pushed her hair out of her eyes while the streetcar shrieked and clanged and swayed across the city.

At the Humane Society shelter we walked down a hallway lined with cages. I was quiet and Mom was tired. Come on, she kept saying. We looked at wiggly dogs and growly dogs and mournful dogs. They all came up to me and barked, and I didn't want any of them. "Come on," said Mom. "How about this one. Her name is Lucky. Isn't she sweet? Look at her big eyes. How about Lucky?"

I shook my head.

Lots of barking and whining. Pain, anger, dog poop. I hated it. And then I saw a ball of black and brown, curled up at the back of a cage near the door. I bent closer, and he opened an eye and smiled at me.

He didn't come over. A careful dog. And because he didn't come over, I stayed and watched him. He breathed quietly, his whole body rising and falling on each breath.

The lady from the shelter said something to Mom.

The big dog in the cage next door was baying at me. Loud, angry, repetitive. Like a stupid toy making its one noise over and over.

Casey smiled a secret little smile. I got down on my knees. Put out my hand.

There were tags on the front of the cages, with the names on them.

"Casey." I read the tag aloud.

The dog perked up. Still cautious.

"Casey," I said again. Quieter. Just him and me. He came over slowly, taking hesitant little steps. He knew his name.

He smiled at me, showing his chipped tooth.

I carried Casey out of the shelter and put him on the seat next to me on the streetcar ride home. Mom sat behind us. I whispered in his ear on the way home. *Casey*, I said, over and over. *Casey*.

We got off the streetcar a stop early, opposite the pet store, and bought food and bowls and another leash. When we got home, Izzy said he was stupid and smelly and a pain, and that she was not going to walk him. I didn't mind. He was my dog.

He slept in my room from the start. His blanket was by my bed. When Mom came in to check on me, Casey got up and stood with his head on one side. It looked like the two of them were saying goodnight to me together. Mom cried. I guess she was relieved I finally found a dog I liked.

I guess.

↑2

I landed with a heavy thump. Back to reality. I climbed the ladder, heavy in heart and body, and banged my head on the grating.

I didn't see the seriousness of the situation right away. What the heck, I thought. And lifted my hand. Of course the grating didn't move. I pushed again, using all my strength. Nothing. The grating fit tight on the drain, as it was supposed to. I remembered how hard it had been to lever it off with the hockey stick. Okay, this was serious now. I clung to the ladder and raised my voice.

"Hey!"

It was getting harder to make out the blackness of the bars against the purple twilight sky. I felt like someone was sitting on my chest. I wasn't scared. I was—something else. I pushed upward as hard as I could. Banged my hands on the bars.

"HELP!!" I shouted. And again, "HEY, HELP!"

My voice echoing.

"What is it? Who's there?"

I heard footsteps, and a girl called out. "Mouse? That you?"

Lisa's face at the grating.

"Get me out of here," I said. "Get a hockey stick or something like that. Long and thin and strong. Do you have a hockey stick?"

She laughed. "Listen to you," she said.

I waited. Was she going to get a stick? No. Stupid girl. She was trying to lift it straight up. I could make out her fingers on the underside of the bars. Her breath was coming in gasps.

The grate shifted slightly. Huh.

"Hang on!" I climbed up another rung, ducking my head so that my shoulders and back were against the underside of the grating.

"Now!" I said, lifting with my legs.

The thing began to move. I pressed harder. We got the grate up high enough to slide it to one side. Lisa let go and stood up, gasping.

"Thanks," I said. We were walking home together. She was chewing gum. I felt better, the weight off my chest.

"I'm going to stop calling you Mouse," she said. "You got all bossy there. I think you must like me or something."

I took a careful breath.

"How did you get down the hole, anyway? I didn't even know there was a sewer there. I was walking through the park, and I heard a voice rising out of the ground. Like a spirit, you know? Only it was you, Mouse."

The workman I'd seen here yesterday, with the hard hat. He must have checked this part of the vacant lot, found the open drain and put the lid on.

"I fell in," I said. "It was an open hole."

"But you're okay now?"

"Yeah."

We came to her place.

"You going to cross the street, Fred?"

My hands were clenched in my pockets. Something inside me going *BOOM*.

"You going to beat me up if I don't?" I said.

She shook her head.

"I don't know why I said that, back when I first moved here, about not walking on my sidewalk. Pretty dumb, huh? You can walk here anytime, Fred. You can even come inside. You want to?"

"I, uh, should be going home."

"Sure."

She spat out her gum and turned up the front walk to her house.

↑3

Mom had an announcement at dinner.

"I'm going to Montreal," she said. "There's a conference. I'll be gone for two nights. You'll have a babysitter—a college girl who will sleep over. Her name is Elvira. She'll be in charge when she's here. When she's not here, Isabel will be in charge."

I took a moment to digest that. Mom was leaving us.

"Huh," I said.

Izzy wanted to know why we needed a babysitter at all. "I'm fourteen," she said. "I can look after Fred. I'm legal."

"Not overnight," said Mom. "That's too much responsibility when you're fourteen."

"What about Grandma?"

"Mother lives too far away."

Izzy and Mom looked at each other. I could tell that Izzy wanted to say something but didn't.

"Our babysitter's name is Elvira?" I said.

"Yes," said Mom.

"That's a stupid name."

We were watching TV in the living room after supper. *Durango Bot*. You know—*The bot you love to hate*? I put my hand down without thinking so Casey could sniff it. Of course he wasn't there.

Izzy and I got up to pee at the same time. I called first to the bathroom. She said no way. We ran up the stairs together, shoving. I got my hand on the bathroom door first. She pulled me back. We fell on the floor together and started fighting. Seriously, punching and kicking and everything. She pulled my hair. I swore at her. She kicked me in the knee. It hurt like anything. I punched her, which is hard to do when you're lying down. She screamed at me, calling me Harry. She cocked her fist, drew back and punched me, only she missed and hit the door frame behind me instead.

"Owwwww."

She sat with her hand in her lap and her face screwed up in a knot.

"Owwwww."

Mom came up from the kitchen to ask what was going on.

"Owwwww. My hand is killing me," said Izzy.

Mom went back downstairs to get some ice. I helped Izzy to her feet.

"Why did you call me Harry?" I asked.

She made a face.

"Did I? Sorry."

"You mean Harry the Horse, right? Why are you mad at your boyfriend?"

"He's not my boyfriend anymore."

She went downstairs.

My urge to pee came back. I'd forgotten all about it.

Izzy had punched me because she was mad at Harry. Okay. So why had I been fighting her? It wasn't just the bathroom. I was mad too. But why?

I didn't know.

14

"What's the matter?" asked Freddie.

"Huh? Nothing."

"Sure there is."

We were walking down by the lake with Casey between us, Freddie and I. It was a little early in the season for boats, but the path was full of skateboarders, joggers and those people who walk fast with their hips swinging out. Man, they look stupid. I was wearing a pair of mirror sunglasses I'd picked up from the Goodwill store on Roncesvalles (my Roncesvalles—the right-side-up one) for two dollars. They changed my face. With them on I looked different from Freddie.

I had Casey's leash. He was pulling, the way he does, wanting to run after every seagull and smell every piece of garbage. I found that I actually resented the constant tug on my arm. Yeah, resented.

"Stop it, Casey," I said, and yanked him away from a french fry.

"See," said Freddie. "Something's wrong."

We got to the park with the dinosaurs. One of my favorite places along the lakefront. We'd come here a lot when I was small. There's a drinking fountain, swings and giant dinosaurs to climb on. Lake Ontario was too cold to swim in except on the hottest days, and kind of greasy to the touch, but you could wade out up to your knees and stare at the ducks and sailboats, and the horizon, flat and faraway.

Stegosaurus had a long tail that made a great bumpy slide. Triceratops's broad back was good for standing on. Mom would cover her eyes, pretending to be scared but really laughing. When we got down, she'd buy ice cream.

Doesn't sound like Mom, does it? She laughed a lot back then. That was before she went to work at the insurance office.

I noticed that Stego's tail had all the spikes at the bottom. The one at the park back home was missing one.

Casey barked even more than he usually did. I wished we hadn't brought him.

I know, I know. Here was this, what?, this *miracle*, a chance to visit my dog alive again, and I wanted to get rid of him. What was that about? I'd missed Casey so much when he died and now I was taking him for granted. Like seeing him wasn't enough. I was upset with myself, but I couldn't help the way I was feeling. You can't, can you?

"Shut up, Casey!" I called. He kept barking. Stupid dog.

"Remember Monday, when I had the dentist appointment?" Freddie said. He was hanging on one of the triceratops's horns, feet dangling. I was trying to leap onto the dinosaur's back from a standing-still position.

"Did you come around?" he asked. "Because this policeman saw me walking Casey and drove me home to make sure I lived there. He said I'd run away from him. That was you, eh?"

"Yeah. Sorry. Did you get in trouble?"

"No. But he did say he'd never seen anyone run so fast." Freddie dropped to the ground, staggered but stayed upright.

I jumped like a flea, way higher than my own head, landing on my feet on triceratops's back with my hands out for balance. My new sunglasses fell off. I swore.

"I don't know what's wrong," I said, even though Freddie hadn't opened his mouth. "I'm mad, but I don't know why."

We walked along the shore, skipping stones. The afternoon sun was ahead of us, slanting across the water on our left, turning it to gold. On our right was the hum of the expressway. The dragon came out of the sun, treetop level, flying right at us.

"Yikes!"

It was a shock—and yet not a shock. Like seeing a wasp in your room. You know there's a nest in the tree near your window. You know they're around. But you still jump when one flies out of your closet.

This dragon was silver colored, like the lame one in High Park. Bigger though. Bedsheet-sized wings.

"It's carrying something!" I said.

"Uh-huh," said Fred. "She probably is."

She, that's right. Dragons were girls.

She turned inland, flapping her wings slowly. And now I could see what she was carrying.

"It's a woman. An old woman!"

I saw her clearly for a second. A dragon claw grasped her around the middle. Her legs hung down, ankles together, knees oddly apart. She wore a sweater and a black kerchief. Somebody's bow-legged baba.

The big leathery wings flapped once, twice, and she was gone.

"Call the police!" I said. "Call somebody! Do something!"

"Why? It's her time."

Freddie looked puzzled. Calm, but puzzled. He had his regular smile on.

"We should try to save her. Call the police! The air force! Freddie!"

He looked at me.

"It's her time," he said again. "When your time comes, there's nothing to do."

He said this as if explaining a really simple thing— not simple like Go Fish, more like gravity. *When you drop something, it falls.*

Ahead of us, a mom stopped to pick up a floppy hat that her kid in the stroller had flung to the ground. She put the hat carefully back on the kid's head and resumed pushing. Didn't she see the dragon, or didn't she care?

She was smiling. Freddie was smiling. The roller-blader who went past me then was smiling. The kid flung the hat away again. And anyway, the dragon was gone now. Like the wasp that has flown out the open window of your bedroom.

I wanted to save Baba, but I didn't know how.

"It's terrible. And I don't get it," I said.

I felt like Purvis Stackpole in math class.

15

I spoke to him the very next morning before class.
Purvis, that is. His hair was wet and his mouth open.
I hung up my raincoat in my own locker and said hello
to him. I'd never done that before, but I liked what his
upside-down self had said about Freddie and I'd been
meaning to be, well, nicer.

"So how's it going, Purvis?"

"Fine. Yeah, yeah. Fine." He sniffed.

"Good." I got out my books and closed my locker.
"On your way to class?"

"I can't yet. Lance told me to wait for him," he said.

"Lance Levy?"

"Here he comes!"

I didn't get it. What did Lance care about Purvis?
He was rich and an athlete, one of the cool kids. He
wore a matching outfit today—black-and-white pants,
shirt and knapsack. He used an umbrella like a walking
stick and strode down the hall like he owned it, like a,
a, like an emperor.

"Morning, Lance!" said Purvis.

Lance stopped, shook the umbrella over Purvis's shoes and made an *after you* gesture. Purvis cleared his throat and sang "Happy Birthday" all the way through. *Happy birthday dear La-ance, happy birthday to you.* When he was done, Lance fist pumped.

"Yesss."

Purvis grinned. "Can I go to class now?"

Lance waved him away.

"Is it your birthday?" I asked him.

"No—but that retard doesn't know. Yesterday I told him that today was my birthday and I wanted him to sing me the birthday song. And he remembered. A riot, eh? Guy doesn't know the two times table, but he remembered my birthday."

Lance's hair gleamed. His teeth shone. His chin dimple winked. I wanted to destroy him.

The tables and rolling bookshelves had been pushed to the sides of the school library, leaving a big empty space in the middle. That's where we were sitting. The library was hot. I was between Mike and Velma. Velma's skirt rode up when she plumped herself down on the hard carpet, and I caught a glimpse of the blue gym shorts she wore underneath.

Standing beside the librarian was a stranger with

glasses, a sweater and a smile. Ralph Brody. The author I recognized him from the picture on the back of his book. We'd read it in class, last term, and now he was coming to talk about it. The book had started off okay, with cave kids trekking across Africa trying to find a lost gemstone, fighting off saber-toothed cats. Then it got dull.

On the whiteboard the librarian had written: WELCOME MR. BRODY. Her name was Miss Cook, and she was old and thin and mean, her voice leaking out of her like battery acid. Ralph Brody was chatting with the kids in the front. He lived in the neighborhood, he said. His daughter had gone to this school. "What am I taking you guys away from?" he asked. "What do you normally have at this time of day?"

"Math," said Purvis. He was bouncing up and down on his knees in the very front row. "We have math right after announcements," he said.

Ralph Brody snapped his fingers and said it was too bad that he was taking us away from math class. "Gosh, I'm sorry," he said. He was kidding, but Purvis took him seriously. Purvis shook his head emphatically and said, no, really, this was better.

Miss Cook introduced Mr. Brody, who had taken time out of his busy schedule to talk to us. She told us to be respectful and to sit on our bottoms and to give Mr. Brody a big John A. welcome. We clapped.

"What are you staring at?" said Velma.

"Nothing," I said.

Ralph Brody did not have a PowerPoint like Jack Stevens, the author who visited us last year. That guy was amazing. He had film of himself playing hockey with NHL stars, wrestling with an alligator, swimming in JDQ's pool in LA and walking on a tightrope. "Writers are cool," he told us. "A writer can do anything. Anything at all."

Ralph Brody took a sip of coffee, smiled pleasantly and started talking about our insides. We all had stories inside of us, he said. "You," he said—pointing at Purvis. "You have a story inside of you."

Purvis twisted his head around, thinking that the author had meant someone behind him. Then he pointed to himself.

Me? he mouthed.

"You," said Ralph Brody.

He told us that before we could tell our story we had to know ourselves. He took an eraser and wiped the MR. BRODY off the whiteboard. Wrote in RALPH.

"That's who I am," he said. "I'm Ralph. It's important for me to know that. I have to know who I am before I can write anything, because I am writing Ralph's story."

He pointed into the middle of the room.

"What's your name?"

"Janessa," said Janessa. Kind of hesitating.

"Okay. You're the best one to write Janessa's story, because you know it best. You," he pointed to Purvis, "will write the story of . . . what's your name?"

"Purvis Stackpole."

"The story of Purvis. Sounds exciting. And you," to the librarian, "can write the story of Shirley."

The class gasped. Miss Cook had a first name?

She closed her mouth in a thin tight line.

"The idea," said Ralph Brody, "is to *know* the characters you are writing about. A lot of the time that'll be you. Know yourself. Tell *your* story. I don't mean your daily story—getting up and going to school and having lunch and going home and dorking around online and hanging out with your friends and going to bed. That's your life, all right—it's real, and it works for you. But it's not a story. Stories are about the part of your life that doesn't work. Stories begin when something goes off course."

He told us that stories come from pain, things going wrong in our lives. "We've all been sad," he said. "We've all been angry and scared. These are the bad places inside us, where stories begin."

He took a sip of coffee. I stared at our librarian. Shirley. Shirley Cook. Huh. She was the same mean old lady she'd always been. And yet she wasn't.

Ralph was talking about sad stories. "They're about loss," he said. "Someone loses something. But you have to know where to start the story. If your story is going to be called *Purvis Loses His Leg* . . ."

We laughed.

". . . then we have to know him before he lost it. Stand up, Purvis. There you go. Now, you can't have Purvis hopping onto the basketball court in the big scene, winning the game with a one-footed jumper. You have to set it up. First he has both his legs. Like now. Then something goes wrong—a buzz-saw accident, say. Sorry, Purvis. Or a case of flesh-eating disease. Creepy, eh? Anyway, Purvis loses one of his legs. Stand on one leg, Purvis. Come on. Hop. There you go. Excellent. And then . . ."

Purvis fell over. We laughed some more. "Hey, this guy is pretty good," Mike whispered to me.

"And then," said Ralph, "he deals with it. Maybe he falls over, hits his head and dies, and the story ends tragically. Maybe he becomes a hopscotch champion. Maybe he learns to work with an artificial leg and runs across Canada and becomes a hero. Remember, a sad story can't be sad all the time. There are good bits along the way. Funny bits, powerful bits. The idea behind the sad story is that you *have* something, you *lose* it and then you *deal* with it. Who here has a dog? Anyone? I like dogs. Cats, not so much, dogs, yes. You? What's your name?"

"Fred."

I didn't realize I was putting my hand up, but there it was.

"Great. Let's do a dog story. Stand up, Fred."

I made my way to the front of the class. Ralph's face was sharp, animated. He looked like a fox or an elf. He asked me my dog's name.

"Casey."

"Good name for a dog. What kind of dog is Casey? A big, woofy, drooly dog? Little, yappy teacup dog?"

"He's a kind of mutt," I said.

"Great. My favorite breed of dog. You love Casey, hey, Fred?"

I nodded.

"Course you do. You'd hate to lose him, hey? Be the worst thing that could happen."

I nodded again.

"Course it would. Now I want you to become Casey for our story, Fred. Does he sometimes put his head on one side, like he's thinking? Yeah, my dog does that too. Do it now please, Fred. Good. Very good. Now put your paws up, like this—watch me. There you go. Good. And maybe pant a bit? Fantastic. Fantastic."

Ralph had me under a spell. The idea of being Casey really grabbed hold of me. I had my head on one side and my tongue out. I looked stupid, but so what? I was making Casey more real. He sometimes closed one eye when he panted, so I did that. Ralph said, "Fantastic," again.

"Now, guys," he said to the crowd in the gym, "our story is going to be called, *Fred Loses His Dog*. It's a sad story—something's gone wrong—that's why we're telling it. No one wants to hear a story about things going well, Fred and Casey playing happily all day long and going home to dinner. That's not a story. But even though you're telling this story *because* it's sad, even though you're thinking of Casey's death before you start the story, that isn't how the story starts. We have to get to know Casey before we can lose him. The story does NOT begin with Fred watching a traffic accident, a truck running into Casey, crushing him flat, and then—"

A red fog blurred my vision. Time passed in thick, slow seconds. I didn't know what I was doing. I saw horrified faces, heard shouts from far off. Coffee went everywhere. My hands were far away from my body, clenched into fists, waving, waving.

16

"So you . . . attacked this author? Is that correct?"

I nodded. "I tackled him. Hit him in the stomach and brought him down."

Dr. Nussbaum never laughed, but I wondered if he might have smiled a bit at this.

"Then what happened?"

"I don't know."

"Tell me what you can remember."

Blood pounding in my ears. Screams. Ralph the author lying on the floor, coffee all over his shirt and a look of total surprise on his face. Lisa Wu grabbing me from behind, pulling me away. My footsteps echoing in the hallway. The long wait in the office. The principal shaking her head and saying she had no choice. Mom's grim face.

Suspended. We left the school in silence. Mom called Dr. Nussbaum's office on our walk home.

"What was this author talking about when you attacked him?"

"I told you. My dog. Casey."

"Talk some more about that. What did he say about Casey?"

I told Dr. Nussbaum about the stories Ralph the author made up—Purvis losing his leg, me losing Casey.

"So he talked about your dog dying. And his story made you so upset that you attacked him?"

"Well, yeah."

"But Casey died months ago. Why are you angry now? What's bugging you?"

I shook my head. Casey was fine. I saw him most days. I came home with his smell on my clothes, the sound of his panting in my ear. So why was I mad? Why did I fight with my sister over the bathroom? Why did I attack a stranger over a made-up story? It made no sense.

Besides, Casey had died at home. It wasn't a traffic accident.

Huh? I was on my feet, with my fists clenched. Dr. Nussbaum was round and wise, a toad in a loud sweater. I liked him. But I couldn't tell him what he wanted to know.

"You still have that keepsake of Casey's?" he asked. "The tennis ball he used to play with. You still have that in your pocket?"

"Yeah." I patted my front right pocket.

"Why don't you give it to me."

"*What*? No!"

"There comes a time when you want to let go of the past. Let go of Casey, your sadness and anger."

"I need the ball."

"Can you tell me why?"

"No," I said. "I can't."

We sat at his round table together. He got out the dolls. He watched as I put on a show. He wanted me to replay the scene Ralph was talking about in the gym, where Casey is run over. He even found a toy car for me. Start playing, he said, and see where the scene goes. I thought it would be funny to change Ralph Brody's story. Dr. Nussbaum didn't get it. He asked me who the doll under the car was.

"That's the author," I said. "Ralph. Instead of the truck running over Casey, it ran over him. Pretty good, eh?"

The doctor's eyes gleamed. He had me do the scene again. And again. I got bored and said I didn't want to play with dolls anymore. He nodded and said we were out of time, anyway.

"Are you sure," he asked, "that you still need Casey's tennis ball?"

"Oh yeah," I said.

17

I was loading the dinner dishes into the washer when the phone rang. It wasn't my turn to clean up—it was Izzy's. But Mom said I had to load and unload the dishwasher while I was suspended from school. It wasn't punishment, she said. She didn't believe in punishment. It was a way to make me think about my behavior so I wouldn't do it again. Who was she kidding? It was no big deal, but it was punishment.

Izzy ran for the phone. "Hello?" she said, bright and breathless, then her face fell and she dropped the receiver on the table. "It's for you," she said to me.

I dried my hands and picked up.

"Hey, Fred, how are you doing? At home, huh? I thought you might be in jail!"

Lisa Wu. Her laugh was like trash cans falling over.

"Oh, hi."

"Yeah, I thought they might book you for assault. I checked the news for headlines. SIXTH-GRADE BOY ATTACKS AUTHOR. You know? Pretty funny. Hey, you still angry? You want to kill anyone else? Toronto has lots of authors. You can find out where they live. You can go to their houses and attack them."

She laughed some more.

"So what did the principal say? What happened to you?" she asked.

"I got suspended for three days."

"Okay. I'm coming over."

"What? No. I—"

"On my way!"

And she hung up.

Lisa shook my mom's hand, waved to Izzy and dragged me up to my bedroom. "It's about the project," she said.

"The—"

"The water cycle project. For science. We all have to do one. Do you know the water cycle?"

"Uh, yes. As a matter of fact—"

"Miss Pullteeth assigned the project this afternoon. It's due in three days, so there's no time to waste. There's a visual part and a written part of the project. The class is divided into groups of two. You and me are one group."

"But how did we—"

"The teacher drew names out of a hat for partners. You got Velma Dudding, but she didn't want to be with you. You know, I never liked Velma. She's mean."

"Uh—"

"Sure she's pretty. Got the hair and all. But those eyes of hers. Mean! She said she was scared to work with you in case you got violent, you know? So I put up my hand and said I wasn't scared of you, and that we would work on the project while you were suspended. And Miss Pullteeth said great. And here we are, together."

She looked at me. Her eyes were shiny black beads.

"Violent?" I said.

"So do you want to do the writing on the project, or the drawing? I think you should do the writing, and do you know why? I am a fantastic drawer. And do you know what I draw best? Water. Get me a pencil and I'll show you a drop of water. I get the point at the top and everything. Here, I'll do it for you. Where's a pencil? Oh, there's a pen on your desk. That'll do. And a piece of paper. There's one. Now, watch . . ."

She drew with her tongue sticking out of the side of her mouth.

"I don't know if you have noticed, Fred, but we seem to be becoming friends. Have you noticed?"

"I—"

"Yes, me too. Getting you out of the sewer, and now working together on the project. But I don't want you to think that there's anything, you know, romantic about this. I like you, but that's it. Unless you want there to be. Okay?"

"Uh, yeah."

"Notice that I'm not calling you *Mouse* anymore. You're not a mouse. You tackled that author pretty good. And down he went. He was so mad! He read from one of his books, and then we got a chance to ask him questions. I asked if he'd been in a lot of fights when he was a kid, and had he won any of them? And he got all red, and said, '*Next question!*' Now watch while I draw this drop of water. It's good, isn't it? Here's the way I see the project going . . ."

She was still talking when she left, a half hour later. I stood at the front door and watched her walk down the street. The air smelled nice after the rain. Lisa's voice carried back to me, getting fainter as she walked away.

↑8

Dear Mr. Brody,

I am sorry for tackling you. It was dumb. I don't know why I did it, except that my dog, Casey, died a while ago and I am still pretty upset about that. Casey was a good dog, and I didn't like you laughing at him. Not that you were, but you might have been. Anyway, I am sorry.

 Yours truly,

 Fred Berdit

PS—Your book about the cave family was really interesting.

That was my letter. The principal said I had to write it. It was true, except the part about the cave family story. I mailed it to Mr. Brody at his publisher's address and forgot about it.

Felt weird, being home but not feeling sick. Mom stayed with me the first two days because—I don't know. Because she was worried about me, I guess. She spent a lot of time on the phone talking to her office. I worked on my water cycle project, alone during the day and with Lisa in the evening. Freddie and Velma had got a B on their water project. The class participation part had gone badly, Freddie said. I still thought it was a good idea. I asked if I could borrow it. He wished me luck.

The third day of my suspension Mom had an appointment at nine o'clock in the morning and meetings all afternoon, so I was alone. I got a bowl of cereal and watched TV. A mixed-up day, gray and windy for a moment, and then the sun would burst out from behind a cloud. At the end of a *Simpsons* rerun, I had this sudden feeling that Casey was beside me. I looked over, and when he wasn't there, I punched the couch. Then I started to cry.

Huh.

I went back to the water cycle project, but I couldn't concentrate. I looked up dragons. A site called *Draconology* had a picture of a dragon that looked a lot like the one I saw in the park. The parts of the animal were labeled with notes. SCALES: FIVE-SIDED, WARM TO TOUCH.

The site didn't say anything about dragons carrying off old ladies and nobody caring.

I smelled Casey. I jumped up from my desk and looked around the room. Of course he wasn't there.

My hands were shaking. What was wrong with me?

I realized it was almost lunchtime at school. I went downstairs and thought about all the people I was mad at. I was bouncing around, all jittery. I had to get out of here. I grabbed Casey's ball and left the house.

Classroom 6D was on the ground floor. I ran across the empty playground and peered in the window. There was my class. There was Miss Pullteeth, pants flapping around her legs, walking up and down and gesturing. Everything was exactly the same, except for the water cycle posters on the far wall. Freddie sat where I did, pretty much in the middle of the room. He looked over once, and I waved, but he acted like he hadn't seen me at all.

The bell rang for lunch.

"Let's have a cheer for the basketball team," said Miss Pullteeth, who was as cheery upside down as she was right side up. I could hear her okay, but I couldn't hear the class at all. "Way to go, 6D!" said Miss Pullteeth. "Good luck to all of you!"

The weather was better upside down. A bright, clear day today, with a bit of wind. I was searching the sky for dragons when I heard Freddie's voice.

"What are *you* doing here?"

He leaned on the corner of the school, in his basketball shorts, eating a tuna sandwich.

"I saw you in the window," he said. "What's up? Why aren't you in school?"

I told him. His jaw dropped far enough for me to see tuna.

"Expelled for hitting Ralph Brody? Wow. He's, like, really famous, isn't he? We read one of his books in school. Is it true that he lives around here?"

"I think so," I said.

"Wow," he said again. "You are one bad dude, hey? Fred, Fred, Fred. So what do you want to do now? You're still all wired up. I can see it. You're jumping around. Want to beat up someone else? We're playing 6A again today in intramurals. Lance Levy was bragging about how many points he was going to score. Want to—"

He stopped.

I think we both got the same idea at the same time. His eyes lit up like flares. I could feel a rush of anticipation.

"Lance Levy, eh?" I said.

We smiled at each other, the same smile, except that his had a piece of tuna stuck in his front teeth.

"We really shouldn't," he said.

"But we're going to, aren't we?"

"It's not fair to Lance, and the rest of 6A. Mind you, they are undefeated. And we're . . . unvictoried."

"When does the game start?"

"Five minutes."

As we ran to the bathroom, I was slipping out of my hoodie.

19

Miss Stapleton blew her whistle and the two teams lined up around the center circle. Lance Levy flexed his shoulders and sneered at the team from 6D. My team. We wore white undershirts over our regular T-shirts. The 6A team had blue undershirts, except for Lance who wore a blue basketball jersey with his name on the back. He played in a league downtown.

Miss Stapleton tossed the ball in the air. Mike and Lance leaped together, but Lance got up a bit higher and tipped it back to Olga. She dribbled down court. Lance ran down the sideline, waving his arms. "Here!" he shouted. "Over here!" Olga fired a pretty good pass.

To me.

"What the—" said Lance.

I was in front of him, holding the ball intended for him. I should have been guarding big Rob, but I knew that most of the play would go to Lance.

"Where did you come from, Berdit?" Lance said.

"You wouldn't believe me if I told you."

I passed to Mike, and took off. Two strides later I was ahead of everyone. Mike saw me and threw the ball. I was all alone. I did an easy layup and jogged back. The whole thing took about six seconds.

Miss Stapleton gaped. The other team shook their heads. The ball bounced on the pavement a few more times and rolled to a stop.

Mike had a funny smile on his face. "How'd you do that, Freddie?" he said.

"I got up on the right side of the world this morning."

There wasn't much of a crowd. Miss Pullteeth, clapping. Purvis, picking his nose. A few kids from the other sixth-grade classes. Freddie was over by the doors. He had my green hoodie up to cover his face. His hoodie, originally.

Lance led 6A down court. He pointed to where everyone should go, faked a pass and drove for the basket, beating Mike, who was guarding him. Paulie, our other forward, came over to help out. Lance should have passed off, but he was a better shooter than anyone else on his team, and a hog. He pulled up for a jump shot.

I was waiting for this. I was five feet away, but the moment his feet left the ground I gave a real good leap. I ended up right in front of him, my chest on level with his head. He never got the shot off, and landed holding the ball. The whistle blew.

"Up and down," said Miss Stapleton. "White ball."

Lance swore. "What is going *on*, Berdit?" he whispered in my ear. "You can't jump that high."

"You are such a dork," I whispered back.

Dupont threw in for our team. He was a quiet kid who moved here last year from Romania or someplace. He had an accent and missed days of school at a time. He got the ball to Mike. Lance was guarding me now. Mike dribbled up court. "Fast break!" I called.

Freddie was right—this wasn't fair. I reached the basket while Lance was still at half court. Mike threw me the ball. I stuffed it.

Someone on the sidelines went, "Holy crap!" Miss Pullteeth cheered.

Jogging past Lance, I fist pumped, slow, deliberate.

"Yessssssssssssssssssssssss," I said. "How does that feel?"

His face worked. "I bet you can't do it again," he said.

But of course I could, and did. The sky was that clear blue that looks like glass. Puffs of wind made little bitty clouds fly. And I . . . well, I was flying too. I blocked shots, snared rebounds, stuffed the ball. And every time I scored, I ran past Lance and pumped my fist. I wasn't usually this much of a jerk, but I was feeling all messed up inside.

The score mounted: 8–0, 12–2, 18–4. People stopped playing whatever they were playing at lunch recess. The crowd grew.

I was not a total hog. I passed too. It helps to be better than everyone else, you know? I'd draw the whole blue team toward me, leap eight feet in the air and dish the ball to someone under the basket. Mike scored almost as many points as I did. Paulie and Tina scored a bunch. Even Dupont scored—an easy layup. Afterward, he strutted down the court with his hands clasped over his head like an old-time boxer. People cheered.

Lance tried to cheat, grabbing me, tripping me. He got so frustrated that one time he threw a punch at my face. I vaulted over his shoulders, landing behind him. Everyone laughed. By now the playground around the basketball court was full of people. Lance's face got redder and redder with every one of my fist pumps.

It should have been a wonderful twenty minutes. Life doesn't give you enough chances to take down the bully in a truly satisfying way. But my revenge wasn't as sweet as all that. I was so—I don't know—so *grrrrshhh* inside, that I wasn't having as much fun as I thought I'd have. I couldn't get rid of my feelings. They sloshed around like a skin full of water. I called Lance names and told him to leave Purvis alone, and it wasn't him I was talking to. I was getting my worlds mixed up. My mom. My sister. My piano lesson. My suspension. My dog. My doctor. My dog. My mess. It all poured out of me like vomit, and there was still more inside.

Second half was more of the same: 26–5, 33–7, 40–8. It was as easy as practicing with Freddie. I ran like a racehorse, leaped like a flea. Mike fed me the ball every chance he got.

Team 6D was having a great time. This was our first win, and it was against the best team. With the score 48–8, and only a few seconds left in the game, I took a pass from Dupont, fed the ball to Mike, pointed down court. He threw the alley-oop. My leap was so strong that I ended up with the basket at my waist. I slammed the ball down and hung onto the top of the backboard for a moment.

The ten players were spread around the basket, looking up at me. By now most of the lunch crowd was gathered around the basketball court. They stared too. Kids, I thought. We were all kids. A playground full of hope. So why did I feel like crying? *Geez, get a grip*, I told myself.

I found myself looking for Lisa Wu. Couldn't spot her.

I'd been thinking of my exit strategy. This was the time. I dropped to the pavement and staggered, favoring my ankle. I took a step and fell to the ground. The crowd was still cheering my dunk. Miss Stapleton blew her whistle to end the game. My team crowded round, helped me up. I slapped hands, told Mike my ankle was fine, just a little sprain, and hopped to the bathroom, where Freddie was waiting. We changed fast.

"Left ankle?" he said from his stall.

"Uh-huh."

"I guess it's never really going to heal," he said. "This game was my swan song. Pretty amazing, though. You should have seen yourself. I thought Stapleton's eyes were going to pop out of her head a couple of times. Do you feel better, getting it all out of your system?"

"Not really. I'm . . . I'm sorry, Freddie. Lance must hate you now."

"Hey!" he said. "Hey, it's us. Okay? We're on the same side. Don't worry about Lance. I never liked him, anyway."

"Okay then."

He smiled. "You say that too—*Okay then*. Cool."

He turned to go.

"Oh, one last thing, Freddie."

He turned back. Hand on the bathroom door.

"Remember the old lady the dragon carried away, down by the lake?"

"I remember the dragon," he said.

"There was a lady too. You said it must be her time. And you said the same thing in High Park when you saw that lame dragon. 'I guess it's my time,' you said. Remember that?"

"Okay."

"What did you mean?"

Freddie never frowned, and he didn't now. But he looked a little put out.

"Nothing lasts forever," he said. "You know that as well as anyone. That's why you're here."

"Yeah, but—"

"I gotta go. See you soon, eh?"

I left the bathroom a moment later, hood up. No one noticed me. They were all clustered around Freddie, slapping him on the back, asking him about his ankle. He was shrugging, saying he'd have to wait and see.

Velma pushed through the crowd. "What's going on?" she said. "Why are you limping, Freddie? Did I miss anything?"

"Not a thing," said Freddie.

Purvis laughed and laughed. "You are *soooo* funny!" he said.

Velma frowned.

20

Mom and I went for a walk after dinner. She asked if I'd learned anything from my three-day suspension. I said yes, hoping she wouldn't ask what, because I couldn't of a single thing I'd learned. I felt different, though. Excited and scared at the same time, the way you do before a big storm. Something loomed inside of me. Clouds were piling up on the horizon of my mind.

"I want to make sure that you're okay with me going away," she said. "You were doing well there, a couple of weeks ago. And then this thing happened with the author."

We were on Roncesvalles. The streetlights came on, but there was still light in the sky. A white car heading north and a gray van heading south made U-turns at the same time, a four-lane ballet. Traffic both ways waited politely for it to finish.

"I had a long talk with Dr. Nussbaum. He says you have work to do but you are on the way. That's what he said. On the way. Do you think you're on the way, Fred?"

We passed a barbershop. There was a dog tied to the parking meter outside. A nice guy with an alert head. He looked me up and down and wagged his tail.

"I don't have to go to Montreal," she said. "You matter much more to me than work does. Do you want me to stay home?"

"No," I said.

"You're sure? You'll be okay with Izzy and the babysitter?"

"I'm sure."

"You can always call me, you know. I'll have my phone on. I can be back in hours. I love you, Fred."

"Uh," I said.

She put her arm on my shoulder and shook me. Like she was trying to be jolly. I stared at some sausages in a shop window.

21

My first day back after my suspension, and Purvis Stackpole was scared of me. When I said hi, he backed away.

"Are you still angry, Fred?"

"About what?"

"Anything."

I shook my head.

"No tackling." He took another step back. "I don't like tackling."

"I'm not going to," I said.

"You tackled the author."

"That was a mistake. Because of my dog."

"I don't like tackling," he said again.

Mike was playing basketball with Olga and Paulie. I hung around for a bit, but they didn't ask me to play with them. One time the ball came loose and bounced toward me. I picked it up and made to pass it back to Mike.

He flinched.

"Careful!" he said.

"What?"

"Nothing." He threw the ball to Paulie.

Sheesh.

You might think it'd be cool to have people scared of you, but it isn't.

What a relief to talk to Lisa. She came right up to me and started in about the project. Was I ready? I was. Did I have my written work? I did. And Kleenex? That too. She had already been to the classroom to see Miss Pullteeth. The Bunsen burner was there, and the beaker and the other stuff. Was I sure I had enough Kleenex for everyone? I was. Her words came tumbling out of her mouth so fast that she tripped on them. Her head bobbed up and down as she talked. She wore shoes with pom-poms on them. She made me smile.

There was the usual milling around the classroom before the announcements. Velma had done something new to her hair. It was shorter and kind of sharper looking. She was the prettiest girl I knew. My heart pounded in my chest when I went up to say hello to her. She told me that I was a creep and a loser, and to stay away from her. I went to my chair. It was a few seconds before I could breathe properly.

She sat a couple of rows away from me now. Lisa slid into Velma's old seat, next to me.

"Hi, neighbor!" she said.

Miss Pullteeth came over to welcome me back to class and to make sure I understood about the water cycle project. I nodded.

"Way to go! So you two are ready to present this morning?"

"Oh yes!" said Lisa. "We have a great show planned. Lots of class participation. Don't worry about us, Miss P. In fact, we want to go first, don't we, Fred?"

I opened my mouth and closed it without saying anything.

"See? We're ready! Let me unroll my poster and set it up at the front of the class, and we are good to go. We have lots to say about the water cycle. And if anyone interrupts, Fred will tackle them and make them stop."

Miss Pullteeth frowned.

"Kidding! Just kidding! Fred doesn't want to hurt anyone. Do you, Fred? He's feeling better. So seriously, Miss P., should we go to the front of the class now? Huh? I think so. Let's get this caravan rolling!"

The bell rang, and we stood for the national anthem. There were announcements about a bake sale fundraiser, a birthday and today's intramural basketball game, 8B versus 8C.

"Have a great day, John A." This was our principal's

regular sign-off. Have I talked about our school name? There must be a thousand John A. Macdonalds out there. John A. and Terry Fox are probably the best-known Canadians—them and Saint Mary.

Miss Pullteeth stood at the front of the class with her hands clasped in front of her. She was in some kind of overall today, with a scarf around her neck and a what-do-you-call-it—a brooch, holding it in place. The brooch was silver and in the shape of an atom. For science, I guessed. Miss Pullteeth often dressed on a theme. The day Ralph Brody was here she wore a man's tie with books on it.

"And now it's time to look at our science projects. I know you have all been working hard on them. I would like you to put your hands together to welcome our first presenters—Lisa Wu and Fred Berdit!"

22

Mom's suitcase sat in the front hall. The taxi was waiting on the street outside. Mom was in the kitchen, going over things with Elvira, the babysitter. Breakfast, lunch, dinner, homework, bedtime. House key. Phone numbers. Envelope full of emergency cash.

"It's okay, Mrs. Berdit," said Elvira. "I can always call home if I run into trouble."

Then it was time for the good-bye kiss. "I'm counting on you," she said to Izzy, and, "Remember what I told you," she said to me, and, "I'll be back the day after tomorrow," she said to the babysitter. We watched through the front window as the taxi drove off. And then we were alone.

Elvira headed for the kitchen. She was wearing a light-colored skirt that made a swooshing noise when she walked.

I stared after her. I'd been staring at her since she showed up at the door. Mom had told us beforehand that the babysitter's name was Elvira, she went to St. Joseph

High School up on Dundas West, and she had been recommended by the people who ran the YMCA baby-sitting course. I hadn't thought any more about her until I saw her in our front hall and recognized her frost-white hair and sideways-pointed nose.

She knew who I was too. I could tell when she winked at me. But she didn't say anything until after she'd cleared away the dinner plates and put out the dessert. Ice cream.

"So Fred, did you do it?" she said, sitting back in her chair and pushing her hair away from her face.

"Do what?"

"You know what I'm talking about. Did you get your hockey stick and lift up the sewer grating?"

I nodded.

"And . . ."

"And what?"

She ducked her head, gesturing *down*.

I nodded again.

"Ha! Good for you."

I had another spoonful of butter pecan ice cream. Mom buys lame, old-fashioned flavors, but even the worst ice cream I ever had was pretty good.

"What are you guys talking about?" said Izzy. "Hockey stick? What about a hockey stick?"

"You didn't tell your sister, Fred? Why not? Too big a secret?"

"What is going on?"

I shrugged. "I lost my tennis ball down the sewer in Sorauren Park a couple of weeks ago, and Elvira told me how to get it out."

"Tennis ball? You mean that ratty old thing of Casey's? You lost your ball and Elvira helped you find it?"

Izzy sucked ice cream off her spoon. That's how she does it, takes a big spoonful and then sucks it off a bit at a time.

"Why's that a secret?" she asked.

I felt this pressure building up inside. I let out a deep breath and looked out the window. Our house is real close to the one next door. Looking out the kitchen window, all you see is brick. You have to twist your neck and look almost straight up to see the sky. I thought about the way Elvira knew about the sewer grating. The way she smiled at me. I figured something out about her that I should have seen earlier. Sometimes I am not as smart as all that. I put down my spoon.

"*You've* been there too," I said. "Upside-down world."

She nodded.

"I said I'd been down there when I saw you that first time, Fred."

"I thought you were just talking about going down the sewer."

Of course the place wouldn't exist just for me. Course not. I should have known. I felt relieved. I wasn't the only weirdo.

"How did you get there?" I asked her. "How did you find out about the sewer?"

Elvira's nose twitched when she smiled.

"I'm not from the city," she said. "I grew up in the country near Barrie, a farmhouse with a barn and a horse for me. When I was fourteen, my dad changed jobs, and we had to move to Toronto. New house, new school. I was miserable. I missed the old place so much. Mostly I missed Pushkin. Riding him, grooming him, being with him. The way he nuzzled me. The way he smelled. You know?"

I nodded. I knew.

"A guy at my new school liked to climb down inside sewer drains. He convinced me and a few others to try it. Jerry's dad was a city surveyor, and he had all sorts of old maps. Did you know the storm sewers in Toronto are linked? You can walk for blocks and blocks underground. Anyway, I started to explore on my own, and I found the drain at the bottom of Sorauren Park. I got the grate off with a hockey stick and climbed down, only I slipped and dropped my flashlight. Next thing I knew I was falling—like, forever. It was like a dream, except I was pretty sure I was awake. I landed, but not at the bottom of the sewer. I was in a hole next to an old wooden ladder and I felt sick to my stomach. Crazy, right? Anyway, I was too sick to care. I climbed the ladder and found that I was at the farm next door to our old one."

"Wait!" I said. "What farm? Weren't you at Sorauren Park? That's where I landed. Same place I started, only upside down."

She shook her head.

"Not me. I was at my neighbors' place, where they were digging a well. The Mertons were always having trouble with their water. First thing I saw when I got out of the hole was my old barn. I practically flew across a soybean field. It was dark in the barn, but I had the flashlight in my hand, to find the light switch. When I turned on the barn lights, Pushkin whinnied. And my head cleared right away. I knew what was going on. I was home. I was where I wanted to be."

I thought about all this.

"Was it the flashlight that pulled you?"

"I think so. It was the one we used to keep in the barn. We hung it on a hook by the door, because the barn was dark and we couldn't ever find the switch. I kept the flashlight when we moved."

"So your flashlight was like my tennis ball. I get that."

I didn't understand how the sewer drain could lead to two places, though.

Izzy's mouth hung open, and her eyes were squinched. She pushed her hair around the side of her head. Copying Elvira, who had a habit of doing that.

"What," she said, "what are you, what . . . I . . . what . . ."

She couldn't get it out. Her spoon was dripping ice cream onto the table. She dropped it into the bowl. Her mouth was clamped shut.

Elvira and I looked at each other. I was still getting used to the idea that someone else had been there. Someone else knew about the place that was upside down from ours.

I shrugged, as if to say, *You do it.*

"There's another world down there, Izzy," said Elvira. "At the bottom of the sewer in Sorauren Park. Just like this one, only upside down. The sewer is a portal between the two worlds."

"Only you need to carry something with you," I said. "Elvira's flashlight from the barn. The ball that Casey used to play with."

"And when you get there," said Elvira, "you find something missing from up here. Something you love, that you've lost. Fred found his dog. I found my horse."

Her face softened as she went back in her mind.

"When I saw Pushkin and realized where I was, everything turned right side up and I had the loveliest time! I saddled him up and rode around all afternoon, down all the trails we used to go. I had just the best ride ever. I cried my eyes out."

"Because you were happy."

"And sad. Both together."

I knew what she meant.

23

Izzy didn't believe it. Not any part of it. Not the upside-down part or the sewer portal or the things that were there that were not here. It didn't make sense, she said. None at all. It was stupid. A fantasy. A dream.

But she kept asking questions.

"And the house there looks just like this one, Fred? Kitchen, hallway, living room, bedrooms upstairs?"

She looked around wildly.

"Just like this," I told her.

"Except that he's alive there."

"Except that, yeah. Casey's alive"

She blinked, turned to Elvira. "And you say the same thing? Your farm was the same and your horse was there?"

"Yeah."

"Crap!" said Izzy. "That is total crap. You're both lying."

Elvira went to the living room and looked out.

"It's a beautiful evening," she said. "Let's go for a walk."

So we went outside and walked down our narrow crowded street past the parked cars and the porches with old people sitting. The sun was down, but it wasn't dark yet. Birds flitted around. Or maybe they were bats. The cars that drove past had their lights on. Someone was barbecuing.

"So the world down there is full of the stuff we're missing?" said Izzy. "Stuff we lost? Do you know how stupid that sounds?"

"All I know is Pushkin was there," said Elvira. "And Fred's dog."

"And what's that about the tennis ball?"

"I think that's how you get there. You keep something that's part of what you are missing—like Fred's ball belonged to his dog—and the thing pulls you to the other world. Casey's tennis ball drew Fred. My flashlight came from the barn."

Huh, I thought. Maybe that was how come the portal could lead to more than one place in the upside-down world. The tennis ball drew me toward Casey. The flashlight drew Elvira to her horse.

Izzy shook her head. "It still sounds like crap."

We were walking east on Wright Avenue. The look of the street changed at Sorauren. Houses on this side of the street, old factories and offices on the far side. Elvira's hair looked silver under the streetlights. Izzy hadn't said anything in a while. Now, out of nowhere, she shouldered me into a parked car.

"*Why*?" she asked.

"What?"

"Why didn't you tell me?"

I didn't know what to say to my big sister. She wouldn't have believed me. She didn't even believe me now.

"You never liked Casey," I said.

"Did you tell *anyone*? Dr. Nussbaum?"

I shook my head.

"Did *you*?" she asked Elvira.

"I told my parents, but not like it happened. I knew how weird it sounded, so I made it seem like I was making it up. Like it was a story, a dream."

The pressure was increasing. Something was about to burst out of me.

We crossed Sorauren. A man walked toward us, pulling a wagon with two little kids in it. The man was making barnyard noises and the kids were guessing them wrong. He went *baaaaaa*, and the little boy said chicken. Then he went *moooo*, and the little girl said chicken. Then he went *pawk, pawk, pawk*. The little boy

133

paused and then said cow. And they all giggled hysteri-
cally. They turned down Sorauren and the giggles faded.

We passed the shoe factory. That's the sign painted
on the brick—WATSON SHOES. It's an old sign. They don't
make shoes there anymore. The bottom of the park was
on the other side. Without anyone saying a word, we
turned in, away from the circle of light from the streetlight. You could just see the top of a swing set and the
roof of the factory outlined against the gray sky. The
rest of the place was in shadow.

Still no one said anything. We walked forward
in the dark, listening to the city—traffic noises, birds
saying good night, music playing from an open window.
I felt like you do when you pull an elastic band until it's
about to snap.

We came to the drinking fountain. The sewer drain
was in the bushes behind it.

Izzy stood next to me. Her shoulder touched mine.
I could feel her shaking. I realized that she was crying.
She said something. I didn't understand her.

"What?"

"I want to go. I want to go."

I still didn't get it. Elvira did, though. "You want to
go to the upside-down world, Isabel?"

"Yes."

So she did believe us after all.

"Why?" I said.

"You know why."

Her voice changed. She had her chin pushed out, and her lips clamped together.

"No I don't," I said.

She pushed me, sudden, fierce, her hands on my shoulders, knocking me backward onto the grass. She jumped on top of me, sitting on my chest, pinning my arms with her knees.

"You know why I want to go!" she screamed, her face an inch from mine. "You know why!"

I squirmed. Her tears, sweat, snot, fell on me. Her sorrow was so close. Elvira pulled her off.

"Whoa, there," she said. "Whoa."

I thought back to my first visit to Dr. Nussbaum, when he asked me if I knew why I was there. And I said, "No I don't."

Izzy was on her knees, tears rolling down her cheeks. Elvira was beside her, still talking to her like she was a horse.

"It's not fair!" Izzy was saying. "Fred gets to see him and I don't."

"So you miss Casey too, eh?" said Elvira. "That's too bad."

"It's just not fair."

I looked up at the sky. A couple of stars were out now. I never understood what was so cool about them. Little dots of light a long way off. Big deal. I sat up.

"Sorry, Fred," said Izzy.

She was turned away from me. I didn't say anything. She took a deep breath.

"So how's he look?" she asked quietly.

"You know, the usual," I said. "Like you remember him. Black and brown, floppy ears. That chipped tooth that makes it looks like he's—"

"Not Casey. Daddy."

"—smiling."

I stopped. Felt something inside me give way. The floor falling.

"You saw him, didn't you? That world is the same, except for what's missing here, right? You said that. You both said that. So Daddy was there, right? Right?"

24

We were on the sidewalk in front of our house. I didn't know how we got there. Like there was a scene missing. There was a traffic jam inside my head. Horns honking. No thoughts could move.

Dad.

"Who do you *think* I've been talking about all this time?" Izzy was saying. "Did you think I meant Casey? I didn't."

Then we were sitting at the kitchen table with drinks in front of us. Elvira had her arm around my shoulders. "Hey there, Fred," she was saying. "Hey, there."

I hadn't said anything in a while.

She turned to Izzy. "I'm so sorry to hear about your dad," she said. "When did it happen?"

Izzy swallowed. "Last year."

"Not very long ago."

"No."

"You must miss him a lot."

Him. Dad.

Izzy was talking about him. Elvira was listening, hand on her chin. Nodding her head. Paying attention. I was . . . I don't know what I was doing. Wondering. Trying not to cry or be sick.

"He was a sales manager. Paper suits—you know that stuff that looks like nylon, zips up? Painters wear them. And doctors. Anyway, he traveled all over eastern Canada and the States. He was on his way home from Ottawa and there was an accident, a huge pileup on the high-way. Daddy's car got hit by a tanker truck. It exploded and . . ." she swallowed, shook her head. "By the time the fire rescue people came, it was too late. There was nothing left. Nothing. Daddy and the truck driver were just . . . ashes. Did you hear about it? It was in the news."

Elvira sniffed, blew her nose. Said how horrible it was. Horrible.

Izzy glared across the table at me.

"So how was he? He was there, right? That's the point of this stupid world. It's where everything isn't lost yet. Casey, Elvira's horse. And Daddy."

I was adding up the differences. Freddie's mom didn't work like Mom did. She had a car; Mom didn't. I remembered her bedroom with all the stuff in it. More than one person's things. I felt stupid for not realizing what was going on.

Freddie's mom laughed more than mine, had more fun than mine, didn't worry like mine.

Stupid, stupid.

"I think he was there," I said. "I just didn't see him."

I don't know how I got to my bedroom. More scenes missing. But here I was, staring at the ceiling.

Dad.

All the things that Dr. Nussbaum kept talking about. All the times I couldn't answer him. The family of dolls I had played with. Mom and Sis and Brother and Dog. And Dad.

I felt like I'd been kicked in the stomach. Stunned, not sad. Well, sad. But stunned too. It's hard to cry when you can't even catch your breath.

I remembered when I tried to teach Casey to shake a paw. *Shake*, I said. I reached for his paw. Like this, I said. *Now shake. Shake.* He yawned. I tried again. *Shake. Shake. Shake.* There was a Christmas tree in the living room. Casey backed away from me, bumping into the tree, knocking ornaments off. He didn't want to learn the trick, but I kept at it. *Shake, Casey*, I said. *Shake. Shake*—until Izzy screamed at me to stop, but I wouldn't. I don't know how long that went on.

Days, I bet, maybe weeks. I must have used up two boxes of treats. Such a vivid memory. How come I could remember the smell of the Christmas tree, but not Dad?

"Fred?"

I was lying on top of my bed with my clothes on, hands behind my head, staring up at the ceiling. Izzy stood in my doorway.

"Huh?"

"Did you really go to this world? Or was it a dream?"

"It's real," I said.

"Are you sure? Because I dream about Daddy, sometimes," she said. "I'm on the highway, and I'll see him drive past, waving. Or I walk into the kitchen and he's there with a cup of coffee, you know? Or just standing there. I'll come in and be so happy to see him, and he'll smile at me and open his mouth to say something. And I'll wake up."

Her hair was messed and straggly. She sniffed like she'd been crying. My digital clock said 9:45.

"It's real," I said again. "That green hoodie came from there. It's not mine, it's Freddie's."

She caught her breath.

"The house isn't exactly the same as this," I said. "But it's close. Your room has different wallpaper. The kitchen cupboards have new handles."

"Wait—I'm there? Me?"

"I don't talk to you or Mom much when I'm down there," I said. "I'm busy with Casey and Freddie."

"But Daddy's there."

"Yeah. I think so."

My window was open an inch at the bottom. My blinds shifted in the wind.

"How often do you go?"

"I don't know. Most days."

"Elvira thinks the place is there to help us. She was sad about her horse, and when she came back from visiting it down there, she felt better."

"Uh-huh," I said.

"And visiting Casey has made you feel better. Right, Fred? Mom said so. That's why she felt like she could go on this trip. Remember how weird you used to be? Teaching Casey tricks? Not talking? You've been happier this past week or two."

"I guess," I said.

"Except you keep going back. Elvira doesn't. One trip was enough for her. You still feel bad, I guess."

"Huh," I said.

And I hadn't seen Dad yet. That had to have something to do with it. I wasn't done with upside-down world.

I lay with my ankles crossed, left over right. My left sock had a hole at the top. My big toe was poking out.

141

Not the whole toe—just the outside corner with the nail. I wiggled it, thinking about . . . nothing.

"I still wear the shoes Daddy bought me last year," said Izzy.

25

I don't remember going to bed. My hair was wet when I got to the kitchen, so I must have washed after I got up, but I didn't remember doing that either. Our lunches were in paper bags on the kitchen table. With our names on them. Elvira was frying eggs.

After breakfast I went over to the piano. On top of it was a family photo. We got it taken a couple of years ago. The photographer was a woman with a lot of gray hair and a voice like a hammer. She yelled at us, told us where to stand, how to hold our hands. "Now look happy!" she screamed at us. "Happy, dammit!"

Next thing I knew I was on my way to school. Izzy was with me. She didn't say anything about last night, and neither did I.

Velma and Debbie were playing some kind of clapping and catching game with a beach ball. Velma wore tight pink pants and a shirt with ruffles at the collar and cuffs. I didn't go over.

Purvis Stackpole was chasing a small white butterfly. He ran awkwardly, hands cupped together, his face clenched in concentration. He almost got it a few times. Other kids moved out of his way, shaking their heads and smiling. Purvis was, well, the kind of guy who chased butterflies. When he blundered into Velma, making her drop the beach ball, he apologized and she kicked him in the ankle, hard enough to make him cry out. The look on her face was empty, calm.

I kept coming back to it. Whatever subject we were doing, whoever I was talking to, listening to, I'd suddenly remember I had a dad. An old man. Mr. Berdit. My past had another character in it. It was like discovering a huge new room in your house. And yet the memories were not there, as if there was a lock on the door to the new room, or the lights wouldn't go on. My dad. I couldn't see him.

I thought, is he tall, like Mr. Sagal from down the street? Does he have a big smile, like Mr. Ottley who taught eighth grade? Does he have bunches of hair on his fingers, like Dr. Nussbaum?

Sorry, not *does he*. Did he. He doesn't have anything now.

Miss Pullteeth gave us a page of problems in math. The words blurred in front of me. I remembered a baseball game. It was clear as anything in my mind. A sunny summer Sunday, Blue Jays and Rangers. I could picture the ugly statues outside the stadium. I could smell the popcorn and hot dogs. Hear the announcer: *Next up, the shortstop, number fifty-seven. . . .* The dome was open. There was blue sky above me, blue shirts and bright green field far below. But I couldn't see Dad. Every time I looked over, he had his head turned away.

"Are you okay, Fred?"

Lisa looked concerned.

"You were pounding your fist on the desk."

"Was I?"

She nodded. "Is it that third question? I don't get it either. How can Stephanie be four times as old as her sister was two years ago?"

"Quiet," said Miss Pullteeth.

"Sorry, Miss P.," said Lisa, then to me, in a lower voice, "It's frustrating when you can't see something, isn't it?"

I went into Mom's room when I got home from school. Where had she put the picture of her and Dad?

I remembered it had a silver frame, and it showed the two of them on their wedding day, with Niagara Falls in the background. Mom had strange frizzy hair, and Dad had . . . I couldn't remember what Dad had. The picture wasn't on the desk or dresser or bedside table. Had she put it away? I opened a drawer and found jewelry—bracelets, necklaces, earrings, pins that she stuck in her lapel. And, buried at the back of the drawer, a stick of men's deodorant. I opened it and the smell was like an electric shock. I burst out crying.

I dropped the deodorant back in the drawer and ran. I was out the door and down the street before I knew it. It started to rain by the time I got to Sorauren Park. Small, fierce, hard little drops stung like flies and mixed with my tears, soaking my face.

I had to see Dad, talk to him. I was scared, but excited and sad too. I felt *everything*. All the emotions, all together. I was in a frenzy. I tugged at the grate like a crazy person. I got it up onto its side, then kicked it so hard it fell right away from the sewer opening. Panting now, I let Casey's ball fall from my pocket, climbed halfway down the metal ladder and dropped, closing my eyes.

Upside-down world felt totally natural to me now. I climbed the ladder and ran out of the park as easily as

I came in. It was raining in this world too. I puffed and panted to Freddie's place. I didn't want to risk running into anyone, so I leaped onto the drainpipe. I got a few feet up and felt myself slipping. The rain, I thought. I slid to the ground and wiped my hands on my pants. Izzy came to the side door and asked what I was doing. I ran past her and upstairs without answering. No Freddie. No Casey either—they must be on a walk. I wiped my eyes and took a couple of deep breaths.

"Hey, Izzy," I called down to her, "where's Mom? And, uh, Dad?"

I tried to make this sound natural. She came into the hall and peered up at me, like I was from Mars. She was wearing the same clothes as my real sister Izzy.

"What is *with* you, Fred?"

Fred. Not Freddie. And then the front door opened and Elvira came in. She said hi and asked if we wanted a snack.

Crap, I thought.

"I'm home, aren't I?" I said. "I mean, really home. I'm Fred."

Izzy and Elvira stared at each other.

26

Of course I was home. Izzy's room had her old wallpaper. The bathroom tap dripped. Casey was nowhere. I stood in the middle of the upstairs hall and jumped as high as I could. I did not touch the ceiling. Did not come close. Yup, I was right side up.

Why hadn't I fallen? What was wrong?

I went downstairs and explained what happened to Elvira and Izzy.

"*That's* why you were asking about Daddy?" said my sister. "You thought you were in the upside-down place?"

"Yeah."

"But—I don't understand. You dropped Casey's ball down the drain and nothing happened? Why not?"

Elvira made a snack of peanut butter and crackers. My mind and heart were breaking, but I was still hungry. I took one.

"You've been there a bunch of times," said Izzy.

"Casey's ball always worked before. So why not now?"

I shook my head. Thunder rumbled in the distance. The rain was coming harder now. The maple tree in front of our house was swaying in the wind. Elvira's eyes sparked. Her twisted nose poked up and down as she nodded. She looked like an intelligent fox.

"Sit down, Fred. Don't pace around. Relax. You too, Isabel. Let's see if we can sort this out."

Now that I couldn't get to the upside-down world, I missed it. I felt trapped here in the right-side-up place. I missed Freddie. I missed how much he talked, how easily he laughed. I missed the way he thought I could do stuff. I missed . . . I missed. . . .

What did I miss?

Elvira poured fruit punch. Asked the same question I was asking.

"Do you miss your dog, Fred?"

"Sure," I said. "I guess."

"You *guess*. But you really missed him when he died, didn't you?"

"Are you kidding?" said Izzy. "He missed Casey like crazy. Should have seen him. Sad droopy eyes, moping around. Not talking. Bouncing that stupid ball. Mom was so worried. Casey was always Fred's dog."

Dr. Nussbaum and the doll playing—did he know I'd forgotten about Dad?

Elvira swallowed some juice.

"Now you *guess* you miss Casey, eh Fred? It's not the same, is it."

I didn't say anything. More thunder.

"So maybe his old tennis ball isn't strong enough to pull you to him."

"I do miss him," I said. "But . . ."

Elvira was quiet, looking at me. A flash of lightning split the window. The crack of thunder followed right away. The lights went out. We all jumped a bit. Even Elvira. I spoke into the dimness.

"I miss Dad," I said.

"Ah," said Elvira.

We stood in the rain, staring at the open sewer grate like we were at a funeral. Elvira held a yellow umbrella. Izzy had a red one. I had my hoodie up.

"Are you guys sure you want to do this?" said Elvira.

I was already climbing down. I had to know if she was right. Her idea made sense, sort of. But I wasn't sure. There was an inch of water at the bottom. Oh, well.

"Coming, Izzy?" I called. I had my hand in my pocket.

"Wait!"

She tried to climb down holding her umbrella. It wouldn't fit. She started to fold it up, but it got caught on the edge of the opening. She struggled for a moment, then swore and threw it away. A moment later we squeezed together on the lowest rung of the ladder. Water trickled and dripped and ran.

"It's a puddle down there," Izzy said. "My running shoes will get soaked if I jump."

I held out the deodorant I'd taken from Mom's drawer. I didn't have anything *from* Dad—a something that called Dad into my mind as strongly as Casey's ball called him up. But the smell of his deodorant had brought me to tears. When Elvira had asked if I had a memento of Dad to match Izzy's runners, I thought of the deodorant stick.

"Hey, you kids."

We stared up. The dark edges of the sewer grating framed Elvira's face like a picture.

"You two have fun with your dad," she said. "And remember to come back, okay? It's five o'clock now. Have dinner, stay the night if you want. Just remember that your mom will be back tomorrow night."

What a babysitter.

"I *don't* want to do this," Izzy said suddenly, grabbing a higher rung on the ladder. "I'm getting wet. This is stupid."

"What about Dad?" I said.

"I don't care. I don't believe you. This whole thing isn't real. You and Elvira are crazy. I'm going home."

She climbed up a step.

"Look," I said. "You miss Dad. Do you want a chance to see him again? To say good-bye? To tell him things? I do."

"Fine. You go."

"I need you."

"No you don't."

"Yes I do."

I couldn't *see* Dad. It was the stupidest thing. I'd stared at the picture on the piano and I could not make out his face. I was afraid he'd walk by and I wouldn't know him. That's why I needed my sister to be with me.

I could feel her trembling.

"Are you scared that this won't work," I said. "Or that it will?"

"Shut up," she said.

"All those times you kept telling me to cheer up. Snap out of it, you said. Well, now it's my turn. You miss Dad more than anything. You're still wearing his shoes even though they're wrecked. So let go of the ladder and jump down. Do it."

"When did you start talking so much, Fred?"

She sounded angry. Scared. Hopeful. I dropped the deodorant and grabbed her hand. We jumped together.

27

It was a relief to be falling again. I'd got used to the second reality. I liked things upside down. I—this sounds strange—I *trusted* upside-down world. It was such a freaky idea that I felt there had to be a reason for me to be there. I looked forward to seeing Freddie and Casey. And Dad. Especially Dad. Actually, I was scared about seeing him, but I knew that I wanted to, more than anything.

I reached out, found what felt like Izzy's ankle. She screamed from up above—yup, her ankle. I held on, said her name, and mine. I pulled her down toward me, told her she was okay, that everything would be okay, that I was glad she was there. I had to shout over the noise of the wind rushing past us. She seemed to calm down for a bit. I thought we'd hold hands on the way down. Cute or what? But before I could find her hand, I felt a blow to my ribs. And another, to my stomach.

My sister was punching me. Not in my face—she'd learned that much.

"I . . . am going . . . to kill you," she panted.

And then we landed with a thump and a rattle, bodies twisted together on the hard, rocky floor.

This was not the bottom of a sewer drain. We were in a perfectly clean, dry shaft, cut sideways like a tunnel. There was a round opening large enough to walk through about ten feet away from us. The sun shone in through the opening. There was a continuous rumbling overhead.

I didn't know where we were, which maybe should have worried me. It didn't. I felt too awful to worry. I heaved a couple of times, picked up my stick of deodorant off the ground, did not feel better. But I knew the feeling—the same one I'd had the first time I'd traveled here. I climbed to my feet slowly.

Izzy was on her hands and knees, hair hanging over her face. She moaned. Her letter from Dad was by my foot. I picked it up and put it in my pocket with the deodorant.

"Come on," I said, heading toward the opening, trying to ignore my stomach.

"No."

The opening was a circular grate, head high, with wide-spaced bars across it. We'd landed in a storm drain. I slipped easily through the bars and found myself staring out at the—wait! Whoa! Was the sky up or down? I'd forgotten that feeling of falling off the world. I crouched for a second, fighting the anti-gravity fear. I was in a dry ditch below a highway. That rumbling was traffic going by above. Beside me were some biggish hills, below me a valley with a forest in the distance. The sun was sinking toward the tops of the trees.

No idea where I was. No idea at all. For sure it wasn't Toronto.

"Fred! Fred!"

Panic in Izzy's voice. My poor sis crawled through the grating. Slowly, grabbing onto the bars for support.

"Fred, I'm falling. I'm sick."

"I know," I said. "Me too."

"But it's so weird. I'm . . . scared. I can't stand up. I feel like I'm about to float off into space."

"Yeah. You won't. You're getting used to being upside down."

"This is your fault," she said. "I'm sick. I threw up in the tunnel there."

"I feel crappy too. You'll feel better when you see Dad."

"Daddy?" She scrambled forward. "Is he here? Have you seen him? Have . . ."

She stopped, swallowed and sank down onto her knees. She grabbed onto my leg. Her hair was stuck to the side of her head. There was a bit of sick on her cheek.

"Where's Dad?"

"I don't know," I said.

"Where are we?"

"I don't know," I said again.

"I hate you, Fred."

28

We climbed to the shoulder of the highway, Izzy hanging onto me like a lifeline. The highway was two lanes each way, trucks rumbling past in a steady stream, kicking up dust. On the far side of the road was a steep slope, a kind of junior mountain, with flecks of shiny rock catching the sun. Warm air, a few clouds. It was a beautiful afternoon, wherever we were.

I got an idea.

"Do you have your phone?" I asked.

"Huh?"

Her face was greenish. I was pukey too, but I knew more about what was going on than she did. I knew that we weren't going to fall up into the sky. And that the sick feeling would pass. Also, I was in charge and that made feel me different. I don't know. Stronger.

She had her phone out. Her hand trembled.

"Call Dad," I told her.

"Call—"

"He has a cell phone. Call it. I bet the number is the same."

I had a vivid memory of walking into Mom's room late at night and seeing her with the phone to her ear, talking to Dad. She was sitting up in bed with her hair in a ponytail. Her skin was fresh, scrubbed, shining. It was snowing outside. I had a cold and my nose was stuffed up. Very clear, the memory.

Izzy was shaking her head. "I took Dad off my phone," she said.

Well, I guess that made sense.

"Do you remember the number?" I asked.

She shook her head. "I don't know anyone's number by heart."

I took the phone from her and punched our home number. I couldn't help noticing her screen picture was still Harry the Horse. I wasn't sure the phone would work at all, so it was pretty cool when the auto-voice came on and told me that the number I was calling was long distance. Upside-down world had the same phone signals as right-side-up world. The auto-voice told me that if I didn't want to hear this message again I should "add one to this phone number." I did and the connection happened. I heard a ringtone and then a faint hello. Mom's voice. I had to bite down not to say hi.

"Could I . . . ah . . . speak to Freddie, please?"

"What?" said Izzy. "Who's that?"

"Shh."

"Hello?"

"Freddie! It's me. Fred."

"Who—oh . . . uh, hi there!"

He sounded awkward. "How you doing, uh, Mike?" he asked.

A cattle truck roared by. What a stink. My stomach lurched. I swallowed.

"Mom still in the room?" I asked.

"You know it," said Freddie.

"Okay, listen hard. I'm here in your world, but I don't know where. Can you help me?"

"Sure, Mike. Let me get my, uh, math homework . . ." A muffled conversation, a few seconds of silence. And then, loud and happy, "Fred! Hi there!"

"Hi."

"I'm in my room now, so I can talk. Great to hear from you, man. It's been a long time. You know, everyone's still talking about the basketball game. They want to know when I'll be able to play again. Lance Levy turns away every time he sees me. I feel sorry for the guy."

He laughed. There was a bit of a bend in the highway where we were standing. A big orange truck drifted sideways as it passed us, and its back tires caught the shoulder. Dust plumed and rolled away from us.

"So where are you, Fred?"

"I don't know. That's the thing. We went through

159

the storm sewer like usual, but we ended up somewhere strange."

"What? I can't hear you. You're cutting out."

"We're not in Toronto," I said louder. "I had to dial long distance to get you."

"Wow. That's weird. I guess these portal things go more than one place. Maybe they link up."

He said something else, but I didn't hear it.

". . . a sewer system running through our two universes."

Elvira's well beside her place in Barrie, Sorauren Park, here. It made sense. Freddie had figured it out faster than me. Smart kid, that Freddie.

"Wait a minute," he said. "*We*? Who's we?"

"I'm here with my sister. This is her phone."

He laughed a long time. "Izzy? What a riot! I didn't know you could travel in groups like that."

He said something else.

"Freddie, wait. You're cutting out. I got to ask a big question. Where's Dad?"

Beside me, Izzy was very still.

"Dad? That's not a big question. He's working, like usual."

"Yeah, but where?"

"I don't know. Someplace east. Kingston, Ottawa, maybe Montreal. You know Dad—he never goes into details."

No I don't, I thought. I don't know him at all.

"Where's he stopping tonight, Freddie? We can get there and wait for him."

"I don't know." Silence. "I can ask Mom."

We were somewhere in Ontario right now. The traffic going by had Ontario plates. *Yours to Discover.* Who thinks up these slogans?

Freddie said something, and then, "I'll call you back."

"And can you find out Dad's phone number too?"

The line went dead. I took a deep breath to calm my stomach. Still felt like I was going to float away.

Freddie seemed different to me now. He had a dad. All the time I'd known him, walked with him, played with him, he'd had a dad. Never occurred to either of us to talk about him—me, because I didn't know he had one, and him, because he didn't know I didn't. We were the same in a lot of ways, but he had a dad and I didn't. Lucky guy.

"So where are we?" Izzy asked. "And where's Daddy?" She was sitting on the metal barrier by the side of the road. Hanging onto it. I gave her back the phone.

"Freddie didn't know. He's going to ask Mom and call back."

Izzy moaned.

"Come on," I said. "Let's get walking. We'll come to a turnoff sooner or later."

I grabbed her elbow and we started off. The road bent to the left, still hugging the side of the hill. The sun was behind my shoulder now. Izzy tried to stand up straight. Around the next bend there was a gas station with a restaurant attached. Cars and trucks were parked in a gravel lot. Was one of them Dad's?

Izzy's phone rang. She answered it without thinking. Then choked and grabbed my arm. "Yeah," she said. "Yeah hi, it's me. I–I mean . . . Yeah, me too."

She handed me the phone with a shudder.

"*It's you,*" she whispered.

29

"Wow, Izzy sounds just like herself," said Freddie. "I could hear her and Handsome Harry talking downstairs at the same time she was talking in my ear. Was that ever weird. Hey, sorry for taking so long to get back to you. But when I punched your number, Izzy's phone rang downstairs here."

Of course, I thought. It was the same number.

"I got her to turn off her phone. We're okay now."

He began to break up again. It was a lousy connection, either because of the hills or the alternate universe.

"Where's Dad?" I asked.

A truck rumbled by us. The words FAST FRATE were painted on the side. Freddie's voice skipped. "Mom said . . . get to Bobcaygeon tonight."

I'd heard of Bobcaygeon. "That's Ontario, right? D'you know where?"

"No."

"Did you get his number?"

A pause.

". . . didn't hear you," he said.

"Dad!" I shouted. "Phone number!"

". . . couldn't," he said. I didn't know if he meant he couldn't get the phone number or couldn't hear me. Damn. The phone line was dead. Damn again.

I punched in the number but didn't get through. No service, said the screen.

I handed Izzy back her phone.

"I thought you and Harry weren't going out anymore," I said.

"We're not."

I scanned the parking lot of the truck stop. Three or four semis, a van and a couple of small, rusted somethings. None of them looked familiar. Dad drove a—used to drive a—used to—what kind of car? What was I looking for? I made a serious effort to remember, as if remembering the car would make it appear. It didn't.

Izzy's memory was clearer than mine. "Daddy's not here," she said. "And I need a bathroom."

We went into the truck stop. The restaurant had booths and big windows looking out at the gas station. Izzy went to the restroom. The waitress poured water and called me honey. When I said we didn't want to eat anything she frowned.

"Well, you can't just sit here. You got to order something."

"Oh. Okay," I said.

I found a crumpled five in my pocket. Enough for a bowl of soup. I was starting to feel better, I noticed. The idea of soup didn't make me want to throw up.

The old lady in the next booth got to her feet. She wore a buttoned shirt and jeans, and a baseball cap with a *C* on it. Her hair was white and stuck out all around the hat. She checked me out before heading over to the counter to pay.

Izzy came back taking deep breaths. Her color was better. "I think I'm getting used to this place," she said. "I could actually eat something."

"I hope you like soup," I said. We smiled at each other, first time in a while. I took a breath and let it out easily. *Huhhh.*

That's the best feeling, eh? Your stomachache going away. Or your headache, or whatever. It's a better feeling than opening a birthday present or scoring a goal. Better than laughing or falling asleep or sitting in the sun or putting on clean socks. You know when you really, really, *really* have to go to the bathroom—and then you do. Pretty amazing, eh? I felt that now, in the middle of all the weirdness.

Izzy hadn't sat down yet. She was staring out the big window, openmouthed. A green car with writing on it—a company car, four doors—was pulling away from the pump. Izzy pointed.

"Daddy!"

Of course! This was his car—our car. Something had fogged my memory, but it was clear now. I even remembered the company name—STAFFORD PLASTICS. White writing on the green door panel.

Izzy turned and ran. My heart skipped a beat. Dad was there. Right there.

Izzy wasn't used to how fast she moved here and slammed right into the glass door without opening it. I had better control of myself and pulled on the handle, and we raced through the parking lot. Dad's car was on the highway now. I pelted after it, covering giant amounts of ground with every step, waving and shouting. But he wasn't looking, and I couldn't run the speed of highway traffic. I gave up and went back to the gas station. Izzy was crying.

"Didn't you *see* him," she asked, "when he was gassing up? Didn't you notice him? Or his car?"

"No."

But I should have realized something was going on, from the way I'd started to feel better. Same thing had happened when I first saw Casey. Really, I should have been on the lookout for Dad all along.

The weird portal system would take us close to where he was.

"What are we going to do now?"

I said I didn't know. She cried some more. I felt like crying too. This was our chance to see Dad again, and we'd blown it. I'd blown it. The world was more in focus now. But I felt worse inside.

We stood in the middle of the parking lot. I tried to get Izzy to stop crying by saying that we could always go back home. She told me to shut up.

An air horn made me jump. A truck cab pulled up beside us. There was writing on the door. BELLE. The driver's side window was down. It was the old lady with the baseball hat.

"You two kids miss your pickup?" she asked in a gravelly voice.

I nodded.

"Well? What are you waiting for?"

30

There was room for three on the bench seat. I sat in the middle with Izzy by the passenger side door. We said hi and who we were, and thank you, and no problem. The cab smelled like old leather, old lady, soap, peppermint. Comfy smells. Her name was Linda Mae, and she was from Chicago. She didn't call it Chicago, though. She called it the Windy City. She had funny names for a lot of things. Trucker slang, she said.

You might think it was a strange idea, us climbing into a stranger's truck in the middle of nowhere, chasing down the highway after Dad. Actually, now that I think about it, it does seem pretty strange. But you get used to strange. Your standards change. This was not the weirdest part of our day at all.

I stared ahead. Dad had driven here a few minutes ago. Right here.

Linda Mae worked the gearshift.

"You crying, Fred?" she asked.

"No."

"I Iuh."

I wiped my eyes with my fingers and was surprised when they came away wet.

We explained a little of what was going on to Linda Mae. Well, we lied to her. It was mostly my story, but Izzy sniffed and nodded from time to time. I invented it as I went along: our aunt's car breaking down on the way to Bobcaygeon, her sending us on ahead to wait in the restaurant while she waited for help. Dad was supposed to pick us up at the truck stop, but he must have got confused and drove past us. Izzy sat on the edge of her seat, peering ahead, willing the green car to appear out of the lengthening shadows.

Linda Mae was going right past Bobcaygeon on her way to Minden, so she didn't mind taking us there. "Not that I believe a word you're telling me," she said.

"What?"

"Two ankle biters from Hog Town here in the Great White North all by themselves? Not likely. You're running away, aren't you."

"No," I said.

"Whatever. I'll help you out."

She held out a bag of beef-jerky sticks. Izzy shook her head. I took one and chewed away at the tough, salty, meaty stuff.

"What's your aunt's name?" she asked me suddenly.

I was ready for that. "Elvira."

"Uh-huh."

I liked Linda Mae. She had a kid's drawing stuck on the dashboard. *I lov gran*, it said. Her tough old hands looked like they could do things.

Traffic was bunching up ahead. Linda Mae shifted into a lower gear. We slowed.

"So do you want to catch the guy in the Cheap Hardly Efficient?" she asked.

"What?" said Izzy.

"Sorry, the Chevrolet? I saw you running after him back there. You want to catch him? Or just get to Bobcaygeon?"

"Catch him!" said Izzy, not looking away from the road. "Please! He's our dad. Can you go faster?"

"Not without hitting the four-wheelers ahead of us."

She meant cars.

"I'll hammer down as soon as I can. In the meantime, what I can do is put out the word."

We started up again. Linda unclipped a microphone from a small box over her head and spoke into it. I can't do her talk, but she asked anyone listening—anyone with their ears on, she said—to be on the lookout for Dad's car. She called it "one of them Cheap Hardlys that looks like a hack." She said we were all on Seventh Avenue

170

heading west, and signed off. "This here's Windy Belle, give me a shout on nineteen."

"We're on Highway 7," said Izzy. "Not Seventh Avenue."

"Seventh Avenue means Highway 7, honey," Belle explained.

"Oh."

"Why do you call Dad's car a Cheap Hardly?" I asked.

"That's our little joke," she said. "Truckers like to make fun of everything. Cheap Hardly Efficient Virtually Runs On Luck Every Time is our way of saying Chevrolet."

It took me a while to get it.

A guy came on the air and said 10-4. A minute later there were a couple more 10-4s and a 10-Roger. The 10-Roger guy said he was Diver Dan. Linda said hi and asked what his 20 was. He said he was heading east on Seventh on the way to the Swamp and would give a shout if he saw the green Chev.

She was smiling as she hung up her CB receiver. I thanked her for her help.

"Huh. We'll see if anyone spots him."

"Why do you call yourself Windy Belle?" I asked.

"It's my handle, my road name. Most truckers are guys and I'm not, so I'm Belle. And Chicago is called Windy or the Windy or the Windy City. Diver Dan is from the Peg—that's Winnipeg."

"You know him?"

"Dan? Sure. We've been talking for years."

She sped up.

"Why don't you call Chicago, Chicago?" I asked. "And Winnipeg, Winnipeg?"

"Well, what fun would that be?"

I chewed my beef jerky, thinking about the people out there looking for Dad. I had a lot of catching up to do. I'd blocked him out of my mind so that I didn't miss him. Izzy must have been missing him all along. Mom too. Now we'd got to a place where Dad was alive, and all these people were helping us look for him. We couldn't miss him again.

Nothing much happened for a bit. This part of the highway climbed and dipped past forest and rocks, curving around bigger hills. The direction indicator on the dash said W for a while, and then SW, and then W again. The sun went from in front of us to being on our right side, getting lower and lower. It would disappear behind a faraway hill and then reappear when we got to a flatter stretch of country. It did that three or four times, like a series of sunsets and sunrises.

Linda Mae noticed it too. "Sun's playing peeka-boo," she said. I liked that.

Considering all the super weird stuff that was about to happen, this hour in Linda Mae's truck—and that's all it was—was about the quietest, most relaxed time Izzy and I had in upside-down world. I didn't know it at the time, of course. I sat on the edge of my seat, thinking, *I don't believe it*, and, *Isn't this amazing*, and, *Holy crap.* And, *Please. Please, please, please.*

One worrying thing was Izzy's phone. There was no service here in the hills, so we couldn't get through to Freddie. Izzy stopped trying when her phone beeped, meaning that it was running out of power. She powered off and held her phone in her lap, rocking forward and back, eyes on the road ahead.

Linda Mae drove fast, honking to get cars out of her way. She used the CB to ask for help. She'd say where we were—her 20, she called it—and ask if anyone had seen any bears.

We had a couple of false alarms. Another Chevrolet driver came on air himself, calling himself Plazmic. Not Dad. A trucker named Buckeye reported a Cheap Hardly with a blown tire at the side of the road up ahead. We slowed, but it wasn't Dad's. Buckeye was a few miles ahead of us. He came on a minute later and told Linda Mae to brush her teeth and comb her hair. She geared down quickly.

"What's wrong?" Izzy asked.

"Bears on the prowl," she said. A small smile

crossed her face as we rounded the next bend and saw two police cars in a row at the side of the highway. A speed trap.

"Not this time," she muttered.

"Bears means police?"

"Course. Where you from, Fred?"

"Yeah, Fred," said Izzy. "Everyone knows about bears."

Around the next bend we sped up again. The truck was roaring along. Cars pulled out of our way when we got close to them. Exciting.

"Is this hammer down?" I said.

Linda smiled some more. "Toes on the front bumper," she said.

Buckeye came on to say he was leaving. Down and gone, is how he put it. "Preeshaydit, Ace," said Linda Mae. "Keep 'em between the ditches."

"Threes and eights," he said.

Truckers used lots of numbers. I asked Linda what threes and eights meant and she said good luck.

We honked hard when a big orange truck drove past us going the other way. He flashed his lights. Diver Dan. He said threes and eights too.

"All the good numbers, honey," Linda replied. "Over and out."

We rolled down the highway as night began to wrap itself around us like a blanket. She had that little smile again. She liked Diver Dan.

All the good numbers, I thought. *Nice.*

3↑

A high-pitched voice came on the air, wanting to know if we were still interested in our green Chevrolet, because he was parked beside one at the rest stop near the Lindsay exit off Highway 7. "A company car," he said. "Writing on the side reads STAFFORD PLASTICS." Izzy sat up straight.

Izzy grabbed my arm. "It's Daddy!" she whispered. "Daddy!"

Linda Mae told the caller it was a big 10-4. "That's our guy," she said. "Can you wait for us at the pickle park?"

But there was some kind of alarm and he had to go. *Sorry*, he said. *Done and gone*, he said.

Linda Mae pulled out to pass an RV. I asked her if there was anything wrong. She didn't reply. Izzy still had a hold on my arm. I could feel her trembling with anticipation. Me too. Dad. Dad. *Be there*, I thought. *Be what I need you to be*—whatever that is.

I thought about the time Dr. Nussbaum sat me at his round table and had me draw my family. *Put in everyone*, he said, which I thought was funny. A sunny afternoon—the window frame made a shadow across the blank paper. *Why is Casey so big?* he asked when I'd finished. It looked like the dog was carrying me. I guess he was a little big. *I don't know*, I said.

REST AREA AHEAD, said the sign. Linda Mae pulled into the right-hand lane. Someone came on the CB radio with a 10-33—an emergency. There was a giant accident—a mile-high mess 'em-up, he called it—a few miles ahead of us. He sounded pretty calm about it, considering it was an emergency. *Better back 'em up*, everybody, he said.

The rest area parking lot was deserted. No green Chevrolet.

"Don't worry," said Linda Mae. "Your daddy won't be far away. He'll be slowed down by that accident."

Neither of us replied.

The sun was staying below the hill line now, but there was still light in the air. It was hard to judge distances. A car coming toward us would be far off, and then in an instant, it'd be right beside us, close enough to read the license plate.

Two police cars behind us. Linda Mae pulled into the right-hand lane to let them pass. No sirens, no real rush. One of the drivers put a hand out the window to wave thank you to us.

I had a horrible thought. So horrible I couldn't stop thinking about it. My dad died in a big accident. What if that was what was happening here? There was an accident up ahead, and Dad was driving toward it. My dad—the only one I had. What if he was about to die right now? What if I saw it happen?

Horrible.

We rounded a sharp bend and there it was, spread in front of us like a lawn sale of broken toys—two lanes of highway littered with flashing lights and stopped cars. Linda Mae jammed on the brakes. I felt the seat belt bite into my chest. Linda Mae took down her CB and asked if anyone else in this parking lot had their ears on, and did they see Dad's car. No answer. She put the truck in neutral, gave me a Kleenex. I balled it up in my hand.

"There!" cried Izzy.

She pointed way up ahead. A tanker truck and a car were turned sideways, blocking the road. Looked like the tanker had smashed into the back of a car. In the twilight I couldn't tell what color the car was, but it looked dark.

Horrible.

Izzy opened the passenger side door and leaped out. I slid after her. Before I jumped, Linda Mae grabbed my arm.

"I'm sure you'll find him," she said.

"Yeah," I said. And jumped.

That was the last I saw of her. I wish I'd said a proper good-bye, taken a second or two to tell her how much I appreciated everything she'd done. But I was distracted at the time. I'm sure she understood. I think about her now and then—Windy Belle, with her funny talk and her big heart. If I ever see her truck cab stopped somewhere, I'll knock on the door and say, *You don't know me, but you were very kind to me in another world. Thanks.*

I followed Izzy's flapping red shoes along the side of the highway, past the stopped cars and radio static and flashing lights.

We were the only ones running. Knots of people talked. Police officers pointed. Nobody seemed very worried, even though there were lots of dents and broken glass, even though there was a smell of gasoline that got stronger as we ran.

Izzy was getting used to being lighter and faster than usual. When a police officer smiled and put up his hand to stop her, Izzy jumped right over him. I followed suit. We were getting close.

Dad's accident had been like this. A highway in Ontario, a smash with a tanker truck. Was he going to die here and now? Was he dead? Couldn't be. Casey was alive in this world. Dad had to be too. Had to be!

There'd been a fire in our world—the tanker that ran into Dad had exploded. That hadn't happened here. Or not yet.

The tanker part of the truck was leaking from where another car had smashed into it from behind. We ran to the car—the green car—the green four-door Chevrolet. The trunk was smashed into the tanker's front bumper. The driver's side door of the car was open.

A figure slumped lifelessly over the wheel.

32

We stopped running. The driver was still. So still. Izzy grabbed my arm.

"He's . . . he's . . ." She swallowed. "This is . . . it. How it happened." She swallowed again. "Five minutes late. I didn't . . . You said . . ."

She slumped down onto the shoulder of the highway and let her head fall forward. I sank down next to her.

"You said . . . you said . . . this was the place for lost things. So I was hopeful, you know? And this . . . Dad . . ."

She lifted her head and a long wordless *thing* came out of her mouth. Not a yell or a scream or a shout but all of them together.

I waited til she finished. Then I said, "Yeah."

The gasoline smell was everywhere. The tanker could go at any minute. I was too upset to care. So it exploded, so what?

And then the driver moved.

His arm lifted off the wheel and fell against the seat. He turned his head to face Izzy and me. And his eyes were open. He was alive. Dad was alive. Of course he was. I should have had more faith in the upside-down world. Izzy ran over to hug him.

I held back. For a year I had had no father, and no memory of one. And now here he was, alive. I felt shy.

Dad. My dad.

Izzy was on her knees by the driver's side door and had her hand on Dad's arm. She was talking to him, patting him, telling him how happy she was to see him, how he was going to be fine. He heard her. He blinked and opened his eyes. And smiled.

"Hi there, you two. What are you doing here?"

I can't tell you what it was like to hear him say this, this normal thing. To see his eyebrows go up, his lips start to widen into a smile.

Can't tell you.

"Hi," I said. "Hi Dad."

A flash of light made me look up. The sun was behind a hill off to the left, and its rays caught something overhead.

I'd seen that kind of flash before.

There was another smell to go alongside the gasoline. Smoke. There was a whiff of something sharp and metallic. Izzy looked up and swore loudly. I didn't blame her. The dragon circled lower. And the closer this one got, the scarier she looked.

"What's wrong?" said Dad, who still seemed a little woozy. He looked up and nodded.

"Oh," he said.

Leathery wings spread wide, the dragon came in to land. She beat the air to stay still for a second, then dropped with heavy thump. The ground shook.

Remember the dragon Freddie helped in High Park? Trapped in the tree root, hissing and steaming, almost cute? This dragon wasn't like that. Not like the dragon I saw by the lake either—the one carrying away the old baba.

No. This was the sort of dragon that devastated towns. She was black, not silver. And she was as big as a house, dirty and smelly and mean-looking. Her eyes blazed like bonfires. The dry grass around her claws smoldered and blackened. She walked around the back of the car, leaving smoking footprints.

Dad was struggling out of the driver's seat. His face was calm, resigned. He waved at the dragon. The way you wave to a friend—*over here.*

"What are you doing, Daddy?" Izzy asked him.

"When your time comes," said Dad, "there's nothing to do."

Freddie had said the same thing. What did Dad mean? His time had come?

"NO!"

I shouted the word. The dragon was on the passenger side of the car. I ran around to face her, too mad to care how much danger I was in. Or how ridiculous I looked. Anger does that to you. We'd come all this way, Izzy and I. We'd found our dad. We were not going to lose him now.

"NO," I shouted again. "GO away, you stupid dragon! DO NOT take my dad. It is NOT his time."

You know how a dog puts its head on one side, like it's thinking something out? Casey does that—did that. The dragon did it too. Wisps of smoke or steam came out her snout.

"SHOO!" I yelled. "Go on, get out of here!"

I waved my hands over my head like—well, like an idiot. And—would you believe it—she went. Flapping her jetliner-sized wings, she took off, lifting straight up, but angled a bit, tail dragging.

I went back around to the driver side of the car. Dad was still behind the wheel.

"Why'd you do that, Buddy?" he asked me.

I almost broke down. Dad used to ask me just that question, in just that tone of voice, when he didn't understand something I'd done.

"I don't want you to go," I told him. "I don't want the dragon to take you—wherever they take you."

"But it's my time."

184

"No it isn't. It isn't!"

I wiped my eyes. My heart filled up like a sponge. I couldn't breathe right.

"You never told me there were dragons, Fred," Izzy whispered.

"Yeah. Did you see me scare it away? Did you? I yelled shoo and it went. Like that!"

My heart was going like a hammer. I wasn't used to saving the day.

Izzy squatted next to the car, stroking Dad's arm and looking at me. "Can we," she asked, "I mean can we maybe take him—"

She stopped.

"Home?" I said. "Can we take him back? Is that what you mean?"

"I know it's stupid. Even if we got him there, what would Mom think? What would everybody think? It's just . . ." Her voice trickled away into a sigh, like the last of the water draining out of the sink.

I'd never thought to take Casey back. Why—because it wouldn't be fair to Freddie? That was part of it. But it also seemed to be—I don't know—unnatural. Against the rules. Cheating the universe. Somehow, it wasn't cheating to come down here to see Casey. It wasn't cheating to beat Lance Levy at basketball, even though

I was so much better than him—because I wouldn't be there forever. But it *would* be cheating to take Casey home. Even though I missed him like crazy, it was better to hang out with him here than to take him home.

Did Izzy see that? Maybe she didn't care much about rules.

Shadow, moving quickly across the ground. Izzy looked up.

"Get inside!" she shouted, slamming Dad's door on him.

"What?"

"The car, St. George. Get inside the car!"

We got in the backseat with the box of paper clothing samples between us. A couple of seconds later, something heavy landed on the roof of the car, making it rock on its springs.

"What was that?" I said. "What's happening?"

But we both knew.

A corner of the car settled as one of the tires blew out. Metal groaned. A piece of roof at the back of the car caved in. There was a ripping noise, like you hear when you peel the top off a can of dog food. A claw poked through. The thing was inches from my head. It was shiny and black, curved and terrifying. I didn't dare touch it. The fabric of the inside of the car roof began to blacken.

The unthinkable happened. The car moved forward

with a screech from the broken rear bumper. We pulled free of the tanker truck, rose slightly, dipped and rose again.

This was a big dragon, all right, lifting a loaded car. Izzy's eyes were like saucers. I guess mine were too. The car roof buckled and bent as the dragon's claws shifted to grip tighter. We were ten feet in the air now, rising with jerky sideways swoops in between. I saw a line of flame. I couldn't tell if it was dragon breath or if the gas fumes had caught on their own. Up, swoop, up. Twenty feet, forty, a hundred.

The explosion sounded like a long thunderclap. It went on and on. Through the cracked rear window, I watched the tanker below us disappear behind a ball of flame.

Izzy grabbed my hand. Both of us thinking the same thing. If we'd still been there. . . .

We were headed toward some hills with the sun on our left. The window was automatic, so I couldn't open it, but I could see parts of the dragon if I looked up. Her huge black wings pumped regularly, filling us with lift, pushing us higher, farther. Her head on the end of her long, scaly neck stretched out and pulled back with every beat of her wings, out and back, like a horse racing for the finish line.

Finding Casey alive in Freddie's bedroom was an *awesome* moment. All I'd wanted to do was hug him. Same with Dad, only more so. Being with him was overwhelming—a dream come true. But it doesn't take much to turn a dream into a nightmare. Just add poison—or prison—or dragons. This was *not* an awesome moment. My heart galloped. I felt like throwing up. What would happen next?

What now?

I heard Ralph Brody's voice telling the assembly that no one wanted to read a story about things going well. There's no story unless something goes wrong, the author had said. He should try living in one then. It's terrifying and horrible when things go wrong. What kind of stupid story was this, anyway?

33

A bit later and a lot higher we reached a spine of rock with rounded hills that stuck up like individual what-do-you-call-thems—backbones. The sun was down, the western sky filled with orange and red and a kind of pinky-purple. Headlights and taillights lined along the highway in the distance far below.

Izzy noticed the other dragons first. She pointed off to the right. There were three of them, smaller than ours, silver-green in color. They flew in a line above us, two ahead and one behind. I didn't know how long they'd been there. They all carried things in their claws—an old man, a grand piano and a bicycle.

I didn't like any part of this.

"Where are all these dragons going?" Izzy asked Dad.

"The same place we are. You know that, honey."

"No," she said. "No I don't."

"And why are they carrying those things?" I asked. "That bicycle? That man?"

Dad turned around in the seat. His face was so calm.

There weren't as many lines as I remember him having. It was like he was younger.

"What's with you two?" he asked. "Are you joking with me? You know that this is what happens when it's time."

Something Freddie said at the restaurant in High Park came back to me.

"Dragon Mountain," I said.

"What?" said Izzy.

"That's where we're going. Right, Dad?"

"See. You *do* know."

We swooped to the top of the highest hill on the ridge and began to fly in slow circles, following the dragon with the old man, who followed the one carrying the grand piano. All of us circling the top of this hill, like planes over an airport waiting to land.

This had to be Dragon Mountain.

Izzy leaned forward to put her arm around Dad's neck. He patted her hand.

"Dad, could you start the car?" I asked.

"What?"

"I want to put down the window, to see better. Please, Dad."

"Sure, Buddy."

He smiled, leaned forward and pushed the button. The car started. I put down my window and stared out. Izzy did the same thing on her side.

Leaning way out of the car, I could see that the top of this hill was open. A hole. Like a volcano, only shorter than most volcanoes. And the hole was smaller. I couldn't tell how small it was until I saw what happened to the old man—the one the dragon ahead of us was carrying. She circled lower and lower, until she was right over the open top of the hill. And then—

Izzy opened her mouth and screamed. No wait, she didn't. She gasped. The scream came from me. I knew it was one of us.

What the dragon did was, she opened her claw and dropped the old man into the hole. I saw his gray-buttoned sweater and white shirt, his dark pants and his calm expression, for a second, and then he disappeared into the mountain.

The dragon landed on a flat rocky bit near the hole and flapped her wings lazily, the way a butterfly will.

Now the dragon carrying the piano was circling lower.

Izzy grabbed Dad.

"Did you see?" she shouted. "Did you see what happened there?"

Dad nodded. He didn't seem to be aware that she was shouting in his ear.

"Well—well—it's awful! That poor old geezer."

"But it was his time," said Dad. "There's nothing you can do when it's your time. Right, Freddie?"

He was talking to me. He thought I was Freddie. I remembered what the real Freddie had said when he saw the dragon: *I guess it's my time.*

The dragon ahead of us circled lower and lower, almost to ground level, before dropping her burden.

I didn't scream this time. It was a musical instrument, not a person. Also, I was thinking too hard.

The hill really was a volcano. I looked down when my side of the car was over top of the hole. It went down a long way, and at the bottom I saw bright red. Fire red, like from lava, from the center of the earth.

That was one thing. Another thing was that the hole was small. Barely big enough to fit the grand piano.

No noise. Dragon wings are nearly silent. I heard the piano legs scrape against the side of the hole. The piano stuck for a second before the legs snapped and the piano disappeared.

I thought about those things. Our car swayed gently, the way a plastic bag sways when you hang it on your bike handlebars.

"Fred!" said Izzy. "I don't—I'm not—I don't want to be here!"

I wasn't happy either. Not because of the volcano. Okay, partly because of the volcano—I didn't want to get dropped in. But I *really* didn't like how easily Dad gave up. Freddie too. Everyone in this upside-down world was so calm, so ready to, to, to leave it.

I wasn't. I wasn't ready to say good-bye.

Izzy moaned, throwing herself back against her seat, and then forward, and then back again. The car moved with her.

I thought about a plastic bag on my handlebars. About how small the hole in the mountain was.

I copied my sister, throwing myself back and forward when she did.

It was our turn now. We were getting lower, closer to the top of the hill.

"Izzy, that's great," I said. "Keep doing what you are doing. Dad, you too."

"What?"

"It's like this car is a swing," I said. "Swing higher. Come on."

Izzy and I did it together. We swung wider, wider. The dragon felt it—she clamped tighter with her talons. The car roof cracked and buckled.

I could see the red glow from the whatever, the lava, inside the hill.

"Get ready to drive, Dad," I said.

"What?"

"Put the car in drive."

"Don't be silly, Buddy. What's the point?"

Izzy got the point. She could see the hole at the top of the hill through the windshield. It was going to be a tight fit.

"The dragon could miss," she said.

"Yeah."

"Dad! Dad! Move over to the passenger side."

He turned toward her with a smile.

"Puddin'?"

She pulled him sideways. He protested and then gave in. "Okay, okay," he said, as she scrambled over the back of the front seat and ended up behind the wheel.

"Want to be beside your old man at the end, eh?"

How could he be so calm about it? This whole upside-down world was full of calm, happy people. Freddie, Mom, Dad, the kids at school. All of them, except maybe Lance after the basketball game, seemed happier here. And yet dragons could drop out of the sky and take you away.

When it's your time, there's nothing you can do.

"This reminds me of last weekend in the parking lot," said Dad. "Eh, Puddin'? Wasn't that fun? Steering around the lampposts. Backing up. Remember you almost hit the shopping cart?"

He laughed. He really did. I guess if you believe there's nothing to be done about the future, then you're going to be calm.

But I didn't believe that and I wasn't calm.

"Come on, Izzy," I said under my breath, the way I talk to the Raptors on TV. *Come on, come on.*

She moved the seat forward and put the car in drive.

194

"Good for you—you remembered how," said Dad.

The car swayed forward . . . and back . . . and forward.

She raced the engine.

Come on, Izzy. Come on, car.

We were close to the top of the hill now—a few feet, no more. To the left and right was the evening, the hillside. Directly below us was the hole with a long drop through the inside of the hill into fire.

The dragon let go of us. The roof moved, made buckling noises, and the black pointed talon end disappeared. We were in the middle of the swing cycle, our momentum forward.

"Izzy!"

She didn't need to be told. She had her foot on the gas as we fell—mostly down, but with enough forward carry to get our front end over the lip of the hole. We bounced. Now the front wheels were catching on the ground. They caught and slipped and caught again. Izzy never took her foot off the gas. The engine roared.

I gave in to the moment, to the flow of the story, the way you float downstream in a strong current, the way you fall from the top of a skyscraper in a dream.

34

Being at the top of the hill helped. The car was angled down naturally. The front wheels gripped the rock long enough to jerk us out of the hole. Izzy steered downhill. The bottom of the car bumped and crashed and scraped over the uneven ground. It was twilight, gray but clear. We headed for a boulder. Izzy put on the brakes. Too late. We crashed—not going very fast, but still a crash. We were all flung forward. The hood of the car crumpled against the big rock. Izzy put the car in reverse, and when it didn't move, she shut off the engine.

I couldn't hear anything louder than the ticking metal of the car.

This whole phase—being dropped, pulling out of the hole, driving down the hill and crashing—had taken maybe six or seven seconds.

I was alive and well, Izzy too, and Dad. We were safe.

Safe.

Safe!

Relief was a huge wave that knocked me down and carried me up the beach.

"Izzy!"

I leaned over the seat back. I hugged her. My sister.

"We made it! You're amazing!" I shouted into her ear.

Her smile was wobbly, like she could cry as easy as laugh. But there was no hiding her happiness. You can't hide it, can you? If you're scared or mad, you can pretend—sometimes. But if you're happy, everyone knows.

"I did it," she said. "I saved us."

"For now," I said. Yes, relief was a wave. But I knew I couldn't just lie there on the beach. I had to get up. There was another wave coming.

I opened my door and stumbled out of the car. For a second, I felt the world rolling beneath me—as if I was a sailor who hadn't got his shore legs yet. Getting used to a new reality.

I staggered round to Dad's door and opened it. He was fine. Totally fine.

But he wasn't happy. He kept shaking his head. He turned his body to stare all around. He was a puzzled guy.

"What is going on?" he said. "Why am I here? Why, Buddy?"

Because we aren't ready to let you go. Because we don't want to die.

"Because Izzy is an amazing driver," I said. "Come on, get out."

Izzy was out on her side of the car, bent over with her hands on her knees, getting her breath and balance.

"Car's shot," Dad said.

"Well, it's a company car, right? You can get another one when you go back to work. Come on, get out of there."

"Buddy? What are you talking about?"

Izzy screamed. This time it really was her, not me. Mind you, when I saw where she was looking, I was ready to scream too.

We were on the west side of the hill. The edge of a sunset shone below the horizon. There was plenty of twilight left. Enough to see around—the highway far below us and the dragons all too near. Our dragon. The big black one. She was the reason I wanted to scream. Job done, she'd been flying away, but now she'd seen us. And was turning back.

The wave of relief had carried me up the beach. Now came the wave of fear that could suck me back into the ocean.

Our dragon was black—a shadow in the twilight. You couldn't see her clearly until she opened her mouth and breathed out. She made a wide turn, got her speed up and flew toward us.

I grabbed one of Dad's arms, Izzy the other. We hurried down the hill. The ground was steeply sloping, rocky, mossy, with a couple of small bushes. I checked over my shoulder as we skithered and hopped down the slope. The dragon was closing in. The only plan I had was to keep moving. There was no place to hide until we got to the trees farther down. Dad couldn't move nearly as well as we could. We carried him between us.

I stepped on rounded rock and fell, bringing Dad with me. I was up in a flash, but the dragon was right there.

I pushed Dad toward Izzy. She grabbed him and they tumbled downhill together. The dragon reached for me. I dodged her claws. She pulled up and landed near me, heavily enough to start a small rockslide. She lifted her snout, for all the world like a wolf baying at the moon. No sound, though. I never heard any of the dragons make a noise. Flames shot skyward.

I bent to grab a—something. A weapon. Whatever was lying on the ground nearby. It would have been great to put my hand on a flaming sword or a gun or a rocket-propelled grenade. But this was not a video game. I grabbed a rock. Baseball sized with some sharp edges. When the dragon brought her head down to face me, I leaped out of the way of her dragonfire.

"Fred!"

Izzy was shouting. I looked around, couldn't see her.

"Fred, this way!"

The voice came from downhill.

The dragon moved slowly around me, claws crunching on the hard ground, breaking the stones. She was enormous, big enough to block out half the sky. Her furled wings were the size of a bungalow roof. She lowered her head.

I waited.

This time when the dragonfire came, I jumped forward as well as up. The flames shot under me. For a moment I hung in the air, only a few yards away from her head. It was like I was under the backboard at school, waiting for an alley-oop pass.

Her eyes were the size of dinner plates, with yellow diamond-shaped pupils surrounded by blackness. I drew back my arm and fired before I fell.

I landed on a mini rockslide and bumped downhill on my backside. When I could stand up, the dragon was a hundred feet over my head. I must have hit her— startled her at least.

"Izzy!" I shouted. "Izzy, where are you?"

"Keep going down," she called back.

A half-dozen strides below me was a sideways slit you couldn't see until you were right there. Izzy reached out from inside it to grab me.

"Dad and I practically fell into this," she said. "It's a cave that goes back into the hill. Come on, Dad's waiting."

"Hang on."

From the opening, I could see the dragon overhead—well, I could see her fiery breath. I wanted to see what she'd do about us.

Izzy put her hand on my shoulder. "Hey," she said. "Hey, Fred. You okay?"

"I think so. How about you?"

"I guess so. I'm so *full* inside. It's Dad, you know. It's amazing being here with him, but it's work too. I'm tired. And—"

She took a breath and held it.

"What?" I asked.

"And *this*."

She let out her breath and punched me in the stomach. Wow. Pain and surprise. I made a noise like *huggh*.

"I'm scared," she said. "Even though I love seeing Dad, I'm scared. And that makes me mad—mad at myself for *being* scared when I should be happy to be with Dad. And mad at you for bringing me here. I could be at home, watching TV and feeling sad. So I'm—I don't know—I'm . . ."

She walked into the darkness of the hill.

I watched a little longer. Our dragon was still up there, shooting fire in all directions. She reminded me of Casey barking under a tree with a squirrel in it. That was us—we were the squirrels. Two smaller dragons flew around with her. The three of them flew in front of our cave entrance in a line, first the big black one, and then the two smaller ones. I saw them outlined clearly against the nearly full moon. A couple of minutes later I felt the ground shake. A dragon—probably our big one—had landed nearby. I waited for her to take off again. She didn't. She was mounting guard.

Well, maybe she'd get bored and go away after a while. Casey did when he was barking at squirrels. Meanwhile, we were safe.

I walked back the way Izzy had gone. After a few steps, the cave widened into a room. The air was dry and hot and the smoke smell was strong. There was a narrow sideways slit in one rocky wall. Flickering light came from there, like a fireplace.

Izzy and Dad sat against a cave wall. I sat on the other side of Dad. I didn't trust my sister not to hit me again. The wall had lots of sharp bumps that dug into my back. I didn't mind. I was warm enough and as tired as three people.

"Freddie?"

"Yes, Dad."

"Did you have a—a—good day at school?"

I swallowed nothing—that piece of nothing that gets stuck in your throat. We were in a cave guarded by dragons, having escaped a volcano by luck and inches, and Dad wanted to talk about regular things. Okay then.

His smell was all around me, the way Casey's was when I hugged him. I thought—this is why I came. This is what I wanted.

"Yeah, Dad," I said. "I had a good day. I presented my science project."

"Tell me about it."

35

L isa Wu's zippered jumpsuit made her look like a mechanic. Her hair was spiked and she had a huge grin on her face. She stood at the front of the class and clapped her hands for attention and told everyone that we were going to demonstrate the water cycle right there in Room 6D.

"This was all Fred's idea," Lisa said, "and I think it's absolutely brilliant!"

I stood beside her, red-faced. I didn't deserve the credit. It wasn't my idea—it was Freddie's. But I couldn't explain that.

The plan was to get everyone in the class to do jumping jacks until they started to sweat, then have them wipe their faces, collect the sweaty Kleenex, and wring them out into a glass. We wouldn't get much sweat, but we'd get some. Then we'd boil it in a covered beaker, collect the steam and condense it back into water. Not bad, eh? Kind of gross, but cool too. Freddie and I had run the experiment successfully at his place, with just the two of us, a teacup and a microwave oven.

His own in-class presentation was a disaster, he told me. Velma, his partner, had been horrified when told of the plan at the last minute. She'd refused to collect sweat-stained Kleenex from the girls, thrown her written work at Freddie and run from the room.

But Lisa was totally on board. She got the class up and jumping. Miss Pullteeth was doing it too. The problem was, it wasn't working. Freddie and I had practically killed ourselves to make enough sweat, and the class wasn't that enthusiastic. They jumped and panted a bit, but the Kleenex were barely damp. The experiment looked like a failure. And then—of all people—Velma saved us.

Like her upside-down counterpart, my Velma refused to participate in the experiment. She stood beside her desk and folded her arms. She called the project gross, me a moron and Lisa a loud-mouthed Yankee. Velma went to sit down, but someone had moved her chair back and she missed it, falling right to the floor. *Boom*. Her legs flew up in the air and she burst into tears. With astounding presence of mind, Lisa ran over with the beaker and Kleenex and wiped the tears off of Velma's cheeks.

People laughed. Velma screamed and cried harder. Lisa wiped some more. I smiled wider than my face, and called out to everyone to keep jumping.

After finding out that Velma wasn't hurt, Miss Pullteeth said that maybe we'd all learned something. Laughter filled the room, and Lisa's high five stung all the way to lunchtime.

Talking about my school day, while Dad chuckled and Izzy shook her head, reminded me of sitting around the dinner table. Warm memories. Also, I couldn't help thinking back to something Ralph Brody told us at the assembly. A story can't be sad all the time, he said. You have to give people a break.

Okay then.

Dad was still chuckling. "You always make me laugh," he said. "Right, Puddin'? Isn't our Freddie a riot?"

Izzy looked past him at me.

"Oh yeah, he's a hoot and a holler," she said.

I made my way to the opening of our cave. Could we sneak out? The full-ish moon was high. I looked up, down, around. The dragon was over my left shoulder, maybe twenty feet away, lighter colored and smaller than the one who'd carried the car.

Forget about Casey under a tree. The dragons were cats by a mouse hole, and we were the mice.

I was hungry and I sort of had to go to the bathroom. Not much chance either way. I went back inside.

Izzy was sobbing, shaking her head. Dad was on his feet.

"Sorry, Puddin'," he said. "I didn't know."

She shook her head some more.

Dad explained. "I was talking about next month's dance—the Spring Sadie Hawkins. Remember how excited she was when she asked Handsome Harry and he said yes?"

"He didn't," she sobbed. "He *didn't* say yes. He said he'd think about it. What a dork!"

"That's not what you told us last week. Doesn't matter now. I'm sorry, Puddin'."

He yawned and stretched his arms up. Then he did his wake-up thing, twisting his head quickly left and right so the small bones in his neck crackled. Man, did that take me back.

"Well, kids," he said. "It's late. We've had a bit of a rest. Don't you think we should be getting out of here? Your mom might be worried."

"There's a dragon outside this cave," I said. "We can't go yet."

Dad looked puzzled again.

"But it's not our time," he said. "I thought it was before, but I was wrong. We didn't end up in the mountain. And if it's not our time, the dragon will leave us alone."

"No," I said.

"Yes she will. Come on, Freddie, we all know this. The dragon took us yesterday by mistake. It wasn't our time. I don't know how the mix-up happened. I've never heard of such a thing. But here we are, safe, so we should go home. Don't worry about the dragon. If it's not our time, she'll leave us alone."

He made it all sound like the weather. So it's your time—so it's raining. So what?

He started to walk away.

"No," I said again, grabbing him by the arm.

"You don't understand," I said.

"What don't I understand, Buddy?"

"I—I—"

Sheesh. I couldn't think how to put it. Dad was alive because we *weren't* his real kids. But if he found this out, he'd—he might not—he wouldn't care as—wouldn't love us as—oh, I didn't know what I could say that wouldn't wreck everything.

"I can't tell you," I said.

"I can," said Izzy. She'd stopped crying.

"No!"

"Yes. We have to do it, Fred. You know that. This is Dad."

"I—I—don't know. Okay," I said. I waved my hand like, *Enough already*. "Okay, Izzy. You tell him."

Dad stared at me. "She called you Fred. No one calls you Fred."

"Yeah, about that," I said.

36

Izzy told him everything. She laid it all out—my time with Casey and Freddie, and her and my adventures today. I guess she was right to tell him. Of course she was. Living a lie with someone you love, someone you miss—with your dad—is wrong. I could live a lie with Casey because, well, because I wasn't lying. Casey was a dog. He couldn't tell me from Freddie. He'd wag his tail for anyone who gave him a snack. He'd chase a ball that anyone threw.

Dad was different.

Still, she was braver than me. I'd never have done it. There was too much risk of bad feeling—he'd resent us, he'd feel we had cheated him, he'd feel sad, maybe angry.

As it turned out, Dad didn't feel bad. His expression started puzzled and stayed that way. A couple of times he looked like he was going to smile, but he never quite did. He nodded.

When she was done, he held up his hand like a traffic cop.

"Let me get this right," he said. "You two look exactly like my kids, but you aren't them. You come from the other side of the world through a sewer drain—a world that is this one, only upside down. Your dad—me—died in a traffic accident in your world. You two missed him enough to come down here to seek me out. You saved me from my parallel accident on Highway 7. We were taken by a dragon because our time was up—only we escaped, and now we're in a cave on Dragon Mountain. Is that it?"

"The worlds aren't exactly the same," I said. "Casey died in our world, a few months ago. My name is Fred, not Freddie."

"And there are dragons here!" said Izzy. "We don't have any at home."

"But apart from that, yes," I said.

Dad nodded. Nobody said anything. And then, after about a few seconds, he burst out laughing.

"What?"

"What a hilarious story," he said. "Sorry, I'd love to keep going along with it, but I don't believe it for a second. I can't look at you and listen to you and think you're strangers. You're my kids. I remember your birthdays, your diapers, your measles, your report cards. Remember learning to ride your bike, Puddin'? Wearing a helmet that made you look like a purple martian? Me pushing you across the playground, and you screaming and lifting your legs off the pedals?"

Izzy kind of melted. She opened and closed her mouth, and then turned away to wipe her eyes.

Sharing a memory makes the feeling stronger. And Dad was right here.

"The worlds are really alike," I said. "Freddie and I are the same height and weight, and we both like black licorice. But we aren't the same person."

"But *you're* Freddie," said Dad. "I even recognize your green sweatshirt."

"Yeah, the hoodie is his—I borrowed it. But the shirt underneath isn't." I unzipped. "See? And Freddie can do stuff I can't do, like draw. He's really good. Oh, and his water project was with Velma. It went badly. Mine was with Lisa Wu."

Dad was shaking his head. "You really are pushing this thing, Buddy," he said. "I wish you'd stop, both of you. We should go home now. Mom will be pleased to see you. She must think it's your time."

He was so calm about her. If my real mom didn't know where we were, she'd be hysterical, dragons or no dragons. That was another difference between the worlds. Hardly anyone *worried* down here. Freddie, Mom, Linda Mae—everyone had a smile.

"Is the dragon still outside?" I said. "I don't want to walk right into her."

"Why do you call them her?" Izzy interrupted to ask me. "You've done it all day."

"They're all girls," I said. "Freddie told me."

"How come?"

"I don't know. How come there are dragons at all? None of it makes sense."

Dad shook his head.

"If it's not our *time*, she's not—"

"I'll check," Izzy interrupted. "If the dragon's gone, we'll go too. Okay, Daddy?"

He smiled and said sure, going along with a kid's wish—*Can I bring my stuffed animal? Can we put on my radio station?* That kind of thing.

She walked off.

"I thought you got rid of those shoes," Dad called after her. "They're falling apart."

The cave got brighter—like a power surge that makes the lights brighter—a flash from the volcano on the other side of the stone wall. Dad jumped into focus for a second. Clear enough to have a shadow. I saw details about him I thought I'd forgotten—the way his hair grew out in little wings over his ears, the lines at the side of his nose, his bony wrists poking out from his shirt cuffs. His Adam's apple that dipped like a fishing bobber when he swallowed.

The surge of brightness ended and he went back into shadow.

"Has anyone ever tried to shoot down a dragon?" I asked.

"What?"

"Like the air force or something? If they're dangerous, wouldn't the government want to stop them?"

"Buddy? What are you getting at? Is this some kind
of school assignment? Who says dragons are dangerous?"

"Well, they take people. That's dangerous, isn't it?"

"But taking is natural. You might as well say that
slipping on the ice is dangerous. Or getting sick."

I didn't get this. I totally did not.

"But that's—" I wanted to say *stupid*. "That's wrong,"
I said. "Yeah, anybody can slip and fall—but they can
stop themselves from falling by being careful or hanging on to something. When people get sick, they go
to the doctor. You make dragons sound different from
anything else. Like there's nothing to be done about
them. Why is that? That's not natural at all. Why not
fight the dragons, or at least run away? If you get taken,
Dad, people will miss you."

He looked at me like my lips were moving, but all
that was coming out was *blblblblblblblblblblblblblbl*.

"But . . . Buddy." He spoke slowly, as though I was
learning challenged and this might help me understand.
"If . . . it's . . . your . . . time—"

"Fight," I interrupted. "Fight against it. Run away
from it. It doesn't have to be your time. If the dragon
wants to take you now, I won't let it."

He looked at me like I'd just said a really bad word.

Really, he was way more shocked now than when the dragon picked up the car.

"Buddy," he said. "What's happened to you? You're a—you sound like a stranger. I can almost believe what your sister said about another world."

Izzy came rushing back.

"They're gone," she said.

37

"You sure?" I said. "You went outside, looked uphill and down? Sometimes dragons can be hard to spot."

Izzy gave a big sigh—*hhhahh*—the way she does, and rolled her eyes.

"I *know* what dragons look like, Fred. Gigantic flying lizards, right? Didn't see *any*. I looked all around, waited a minute and looked again. I went outside myself to make sure. There's *no* dragon around."

Dad insisted on going back up the hill to the car. He wanted his phone and jacket from the front passenger seat.

"We're fifty miles from anywhere," he said. "There's no traffic at this time of night. I'll call a cab to pick us up on the highway. And pay for it. I need my wallet and phone."

Which made some sense. Izzy and I looked at each other.

"I'll get your stuff," I said. "I'm faster than you, and I know where the car is."

"Are you really faster?" said Dad. "You're a kid, Freddie. I'm a grown-up."

We were in a narrow rocky gully. Down a ways the gully filled in and the going looked easier. Much farther down was a solid line of forest.

"Follow this gully," I said. "I should catch up to you before it ends, but if I don't, aim for that tall skinny tree that sticks up above the rest. Wait for me there. Okay, Izzy?"

She nodded, took Dad's arm.

He said, "I don't know how fast you think you can go, Freddie, but—"

That was all I heard. I was racing uphill, bounding through the night air.

I found the hole easily enough. It was at the top of Dragon Mountain and there was steam coming out. I stood on the edge for a second, peering down. Red fire. I thought of the game I'd play as a kid, leaping around the living room furniture, avoiding the floor because it was lava. Here was the real thing.

Weird to think of volcanoes in southern Ontario. Iceland, Japan, Mexico—yes. Hawaii, Italy—okay. But not here.

Weirder to think that I came to this place, and went home again, through the center of the earth that was bubbling down there.

So much for weird.

Now, where was the car? I ran around the top of the mountain, looking downhill. There was the boulder we'd crashed into. Right? I ran down to check.

I caught up to Dad and Izzy quicker than I thought. They were working their way down the gully carefully, Dad in the lead and Izzy following.

Dad didn't believe I'd been to the top of the mountain and back.

"You've only been gone a couple of minutes," he said.

I showed him what I'd found by the big boulder.

"Huh," he said. "That's my hubcap, all right."

"It's all that was left," I said. "The car's gone. The dragon must have come back for it. Maybe it was the car's time," I said.

I was making a joke—*How can it be a thing's time?*—but Dad nodded seriously.

"I guess so," he said, and set off again.

Izzy and I shrugged at each other.

"How are we going to get him back home?" she whispered to me.

"What about *your* phone?"

"It's in my pocket. It didn't work, remember. Uhhh— yeah, still no signal. And no power, either. We'll need to borrow someone else'e phone."

Shadow.

I looked up as something bulky and shapeless and metallic clattered to the ground just below us. What the—

Long poles, a cross piece, chains. A swing set? Yes. One of those backyard things. Kids in commercials play on them and get their pants dirty, but Mom doesn't mind because she has the right kind of laundry soap. You know.

The swing set broke apart when it hit the ground. One of the frame poles bounced high in the air, turned over and stuck in the ground like a javelin way down the hill.

Why were swing sets falling from the sky?

Oh, wait.

Yes, there was a dragon overhead. For some reason she'd dropped the swing set she was carrying, and now she was coming after it. She landed below us with a thump and clatter.

Izzy and I held onto Dad. Her hair swung wildly as she looked around for a way out.

"What do we do *now*?" she whispered.

The dragon was directly below us, in the middle of the gully. If we kept going, we'd run into her. But if we tried to climb out of the gully, the dragon would catch us—maybe me and Izzy, certainly Dad, who couldn't jump as far as us.

"Sit and wait," I said. "Maybe she'll fly off."

"What if she *doesn't*?"

Why do people ask questions like that? What if this or that happens or this other thing doesn't happen? You can always think of ways to go wrong. If life was easy everybody would be healthy, full and rich. And smiling more.

"I don't know," I said to Izzy. "We'll try something else I guess."

We waited. Dad made a step to keep going, but we held him back. He was going to say something to me, then he closed his mouth.

The dragon was having trouble picking up the dropped swing set. She didn't maneuver very well on the slope. She sort of hopped and clutched awkwardly.

A little dragon, this one. The moonlight glinted off her silver scales.

She grabbed the glider part of the swing set in one forefoot and tried to take off. She flapped a couple of times, lost her balance and settled back. I couldn't see clearly under her body. Her wings blocked the light. But I made a guess.

"Let's climb the gully and go around," I said. "This dragon won't fly after us."

"What?"

"I said we'd do something else if she didn't fly away, right? This is something else. I've seen the dragon before," I said. "That's Stumbler."

I explained quickly about seeing the dragon in High Park and Freddie freeing her. "She's lame in one foot—that's why she dropped the swing set. And now I think her foot is stuck again," I said. "So we can climb up this gully and go around her."

"You and—Freddie?" Dad said.

"Yeah."

Above the gully was a bumpy ridge of uneven ground. The footing was terrible and we went slowly, not wanting to slip. Stumbler was on our right and a little below us. She was still trying to take off. From this angle, I could see that my guess was correct—her twisted forefoot was stuck somehow.

We made it past Stumbler. For a few seconds, it seemed like we were going to make it all the way down to the shelter of the trees. And then—well, and then it didn't seem like that anymore.

I told you the moon was fullish, right? It floated way up there, right overhead, like a creamy balloon. I hung onto my dad's arm, feeling a bit chilly, worrying about getting to the highway and finding a lift, but otherwise pretty good. And then. And then. And then I took a glance up at the fullish moon. And outlined against it, as clear and unmistakable as ET's bicycle, was a dragon.

"Freeze!" I whispered, squeezing Dad's arm.

She was so close and so big she blocked out half the moon.

"It's coming for us, isn't it?" whispered Izzy.

"Yeah."

She had to be our old dragon. The one who'd carried us here, who'd chased us into to our mouse hole. Wherever she'd flown off to, she was back.

"It'll see us soon, won't it?"

"Maybe. If we move."

"But we have to move. We have to get away. So it'll see us."

"Yeah."

Izzy wasn't scared. I saw her check downhill, shake her head. The trees were far away. It'd take us ten minutes to reach them. Too long. How could we . . . what could we. . . .

I didn't know what to do. The big dragon was high overhead, circling, watching. Izzy stared uphill and off to the side. There was the gulley, and in the gulley was Stumbler, the little dragon with her broken foot caught on something.

"I wonder," whispered Izzy.

"What?"

She nodded. "Let's try it."

Yeah, she thought of it. I'm the one telling the story, so you might think I'd be the one with all the cool ideas. But this one was Izzy's.

———

"Let's try what?" I asked.

"You said you knew that little dragon back there?"

"Yeah. Freddie helped her in High Park, like I said. Her foot was stuck—like now—and he freed it."

"Would it—would she remember that?"

"I don't know. Maybe. Why?"

"Well, I was wondering if we could—if all of us could fit on its back. Would that work? A dragon could get us out of here fast. Do you think it—she would go where we wanted? Would she go back to High Park?"

The short answer was no. Stumbler would go where she wanted to go. But she'd have trouble dropping us if we were on her back. And she might think I was Freddie and remember me. That'd be cool, eh? What was that story about the guy who took the thorn out of the lion's paw? Like that.

And no other option looked as good. We only had a few minutes.

"I think it's a great idea, Izzy. Want to try? 'Cause I'm willing if you are."

She nodded.

So we walked back uphill. Dad wanted to know what was going on. We didn't tell him. "We're going to find a way home," said Izzy.

38

We looked down at little Stumbler. She was in the gully and we stood on a flat rock just above her. A jump of a few feet, that was all.

Her wings flapped. She strained. I could feel the tension coming off her. It was like I could read her mind. She reminded me of Casey, that time he got his head caught between the railings of the front porch. He knew he'd done something stupid and was so upset at himself that he made it harder for me to help him.

Stumbler breathed a weak stream of fire. Maybe because she was saving her strength, or because she was young and small. Whatever, it barely got past her snout. If the big black dragon was a flamethrower, Stumbler was more like a barbecue lighter.

"I'll go down there," I said to Izzy. "See if she remembers me—I look just like Freddie. Meanwhile, you and Dad jump onto her back. It's not far. I'll release her foot so she can fly, then I'll jump on myself."

Izzy nodded, but Dad wore that puzzled expression I was getting used to.

"No one rides a dragon," he said. "No one ever has."

"We're going to," said Izzy.

"No."

His calm started to get to me.

"Do you want to die—to be taken by the dragon?" I said. "Do you want all of us to be taken?"

"It's not our decision."

"Yes it is!"

Dad blinked and took a step back. He wasn't used to me yelling at him. I guess Freddie never did.

I didn't care.

"There's lots we can't control," I said. "Bad things happen. Accidents, luck, whatever—these things are not our decision. But we can decide what we *do* about the bad luck, about the accidents. We can't stop the dragon coming after us. But we can decide to get away."

"No one escapes."

"We can try. You can always try."

Silence. I saw a flash of fire way overhead. Had the big dragon seen us? Was she coming for us?

"Fred's right, Dad," said Izzy. "We came a long way to save you, Daddy, and we're going to do it."

"Let me get down there first," I said. "Then you jump."

I jumped into the gully and faced the little dragon. I remembered Freddie's approach. I talked to her.

"Hi there," I said. "Remember me? We met in the park a few weeks ago. You were stuck. I helped you then. I can help you now. Your leg's caught again, eh?"

The dragon blinked. Her eyes had the same diamond pupils as the big dragon's. I walked toward her slowly, trying for that calm that gives confidence. Doctor calm. A step. Another.

I kept my voice conversational. "*Okay, Izzy. Now.*"

I didn't see her jump. I was watching the dragon. Stumbler gave a start and flapped her wings.

"Good girl," I told her. "Good for you, Stumbler. *You on, Izzy?*"

I tried to pitch my voice the same way, but I couldn't disguise the extra urgency.

"Yeah," she said, and then, louder, "Come on, Daddy. Jump. I'll catch you."

I looked up. There was Izzy with her hands out, and there was Dad above her, shaking his head.

"No."

Wow. I had not seen this crisis coming. I didn't know what to do. I tried to keep the dragon calm.

"Hey, girl," I said. I was almost close enough to touch her now. Her body was low to the ground—I hoped I wouldn't have to crawl under her to free her leg.

My next step I hit my foot against something metal-lic. The hubcap I'd brought back from the car to show Dad. It must have rolled down here. I bent to pick it up. I don't know why—it was something to hold.

I could *feel* Stumbler's frustration and fear. Just like Casey with his head stuck. He'd almost pulled his ears off, trying to get free. Stumbler wanted to fly away so bad she could taste it.

"What are you *doing*?" called Dad. "Stop that! I don't—"

I looked up quickly. Izzy—my amazing sister—was not going to leave Dad behind. She'd leaped back onto the ledge beside Dad. Now she pushed him! That's right—pushed him into space. Dad landed on the drag-on's back and clung instinctively to the nearer wing. Izzy jumped after him.

I almost cheered.

Stumbler startled again, lifting herself right off the ground—except for the one trapped leg. She flapped like a hurricane, then came down again. My sister and dad hung on tight.

Stumbler turned her attention to me. Again, she reminded me of Casey. When I'd reached to help him out of the railing, he'd snapped at me. Same thing hap-pened now. I was trying to help Stumbler get free, but this isn't like that story about the lion. She breathed her fire right at me—a pretty good shot too. I threw up my arm as a reflex. The hubcap acted like a shield, deflecting the flame.

"Easy!" I said to her. "Easy, girl."

I dropped the hubcap, which was now amazingly hot. How did those knights fight dragons without cooking themselves?

Remember the swing pole that bounced and stuck in the ground? I ran over and pulled it out. When Stumbler had raised herself up, I saw that her weak left forefoot was caught in one end of the swing set, and the other end was wedged into a crack on the gully floor. That's how she was trapped.

I held the pole under my arm and poked at Stumbler's foot. On my second try I got the metal brace out of the hole in the ground, the way you get stuff out from between your teeth with a toothpick. The little dragon took a shuffle step and sensed she was free.

"Good girl!" I said to her, and then in the same tone, "*Get ready, Izzy.*"

I thought I'd have a minute while Stumbler tried to pick up the swing set. Wasn't she supposed to drop that in the volcano? But she was so desperate to take off that she ignored the swings. Carrying Dad and Izzy, she needed a couple of hops and some mighty flapping, and then she was off the ground. Without me.

"FRED!"

I had never—have never—heard my sister's voice sound like that. I hope I never hear it again.

I ran after the dragon and jumped as high as I could, higher than I'd ever gone playing basketball. If I'd been jumping at my house, I'd have got up to my bedroom window. I was behind Stumbler and on her left side. I felt a thwack on the side of my head—the kind of sudden blow that makes you see stars. She'd lashed me with her tail. I reached out without thinking and locked my hands around one of the triangular spiky things that stuck up. I shinnied around like her tail was a tree branch. Now I was sitting up, riding it where it joined her body. I faced forward. Dad was right there, hanging onto Izzy, staring back at me with his mouth open.

I reached out with one hand. He grabbed it and pulled me forward onto the dragon's back.

"Thanks, Dad," I said.

I grabbed hold of one wing where it popped out of her shoulder. Izzy and Dad were sharing the other one. My head rang like a bell.

"That was close," Izzy said.

Dad looked from one to the other of us.

"Who *are* you guys?" he asked.

39

Did that whack on the head mix something up in my brain? Maybe. Because for a while after that moment—after I landed on the dragon's tail and Dad pulled me to safety—my memory got a little out of hand. It flashed and popped and went out. Time seemed to move differently, the way it is in a dream, or when you go crazy. Yeah, like what's his name in Dr. Nussbaum's office, with the frogs in the toilet tank. That guy. Crazy. Maybe that's what happened to me for a bit.

This is a warning, in case you're wondering how come the story starts to make even less sense than it did.

Not a lot of noise on a dragon. No clanking or grinding. Just the great wings, pumping. The wind made a whooshing noise in my ears, like blowing across the top of a pop bottle.

Izzy sat cross-legged. I knelt. I can't sit cross-legged. I don't bend well. Mom goes to yoga and one time she tried to teach me some of the moves. Izzy laughed so hard I thought she was going to be sick.

I couldn't tell where we were going, but it didn't seem to be toward the volcano. There were a couple of headlights below and off to the right. The highway.

We flew in a lazy circle. Not very high off the ground. "Which way is Toronto?" Izzy asked.

"Don't know," I said.

The moon was on our left. A few lights flickered a long way away in that direction. Ahead of us I saw a flat dark surface that was probably a lake. I saw hills, trees. I looked behind us—

Oh.

Oh, yeah. Forgot about her.

The dragon. The big black one. How could I forget? Mind you, I forgot about Dad for the longest time, and if I can do that, I can forget about anything. Just lock it away in my memory and forget the combination.

So yeah, I'd forgotten all about the big black dragon, and here she was, still a ways behind but coming after us, like a police car with the lights flashing in our rearview mirror.

Little Stumbler realized this the same time I did. She swooped low and began to fly fast and straight.

Fear. Not mine—the dragon's. I could feel it through my knees, through my hand that gripped the little dragon's wing joint. Stumbler knew she was in big trouble. That's why she flew so fast.

Stumbler the dragon was talking to me? Yes. Sort of. Somehow—some weird how—I understood her and I knew what she was feeling. It's like my brain started to free float after I got clonked on the head, and I was picking up Stumbler's signals. I told you the story would start to get even weirder, right?

And the reason I totally believed Stumbler's fear was because the same thing had happened to me.

When I got my first two-wheeler, Mom made me promise to wear my bright yellow helmet every time. Every time? Every time. Every *single* time? Yes, every single time. Except that my helmet made me look dorky. One day when Mom went shopping, I rode bareheaded. Dad drove home early and honked when he saw me helmetless—a loud, angry blast. And, without thinking, without looking back, I rode off as fast as I could.

That's what Stumbler was doing. She'd been caught doing something she shouldn't be doing, and she was in trouble. I felt that strongly—she wasn't mad, she was scared. She panicked, flapping her wings as hard as I'd pedaled my blue racer on that long-ago afternoon.

40

We passed a lake, a forest, a couple of barns. A highway threaded through the landscape. The cowboy moon rode across the sky. Izzy sat forward, legs wrapped around the dragon's neck. Dad had one arm locked around a pumping wing joint. I was on my stomach, hanging on to a foreleg.

"So you're not Freddie," said Dad. "Not Izzy."

He nodded, absorbing the idea, working with it.

The dragon wings beat silently.

"But you are here for me," he went on. "You came because I'm your father. You're mine and I'm yours. Right, Puddin'?"

Izzy's eyes were shining.

Pinpoints of light ahead and to the right. Not very many, not very far away. A town coming up.

I could see the big dragon clearly now, wings pumping, tail lashing, fire shooting forward. She could have caught us by now but preferred to coast above and behind us. Maybe she didn't have a plan—or maybe she was trying to wear Stumbler out. The little dragon was tiring. Wing pump, pause, pause, pump, pump, pump. Fatigue was getting stronger than fear.

Again, I knew this feeling. My helmetless bike escapade led me around the block, pulling away from Dad as I roared down Sorauren Avenue and along Galley, then slowing as I climbed Roncesvalles and turned up onto Garden, gasping, sucking breaths, forcing my feet down onto the pedals, knowing Dad was gaining every second but caring less and less, nearly resigned to the inevitable, more tired than scared.

"So what happened when I disappeared from your world?" Dad asked. "Come to think of it, what happens if there are no dragons? Where do the bodies go? Where does everything go?"

Izzy told him about getting his remains delivered to the funeral place.

"Remains?" said Dad.

"From the accident site. You know, bones and ashes and stuff."

"Ew. Remains."

Of course, I thought, down here there were no remains. Everything ended up in a volcano. Still, I was curious.

"What remains do you mean?" I asked Izzy.

"The urn we kept on the piano for months, stupid. By the family picture. Remember?"

"No," I said.

"Remember, we went to the cemetery for a service and to put the urn in a display thing."

"No."

"And you insisted on bringing Casey with us, only he wouldn't sit still and kept barking at the minister?"

"No!"

"Okay, Buddy," said Dad. "There, there. I'm here now."

Which was true, I guess.

The black dragon had climbed above us. She'd been cruising over our left flank for a while. Now, as if to say, *Enough of this!* she tucked her wings tight to her body and dived. When she was a few yards off she opened her mouth. Fire shot out, catching Stumbler's tail and causing the little dragon to give a jump of fear and pain, and swoop away to the right.

The smoke was thick and yucky. Burning dragon. No, wait, that was Dad's shirt. I dropped my handhold and helped him bat out the flames.

"Ouch!" Dad stared down at his hand.

"What do you think the volcano would have felt like?"

He didn't answer.

Stumbler's swoop to the right brought us into the town. The black dragon passed us and then pulled right in front of us, acting like a police car, trying to get us to pull over. We flew down the main street at roof level. Nobody out—it was late. The black dragon breathed long, fiery breaths. I saw a line of flame on a power line as we passed.

Stumbler made a last attempt to get away, banking sharply then pumping her wings like crazy. Two, three, four, six blocks passed in a flash. I checked over my shoulder. The black dragon had turned to follow us. Her fiery breath tore along the roof of an old town-hall kind of building. Stumbler pumped some more, but her will was failing her. We were over a subdivision at the edge of town, well-lit streets lined with new houses that backed onto a farmer's field. I heard an explosion behind us, checked quickly. A ball of flame, street level.

We were over the field. Stumbler stopped pumping her wings and spread them wide, angling downward. She was done. I could hear her saying to herself, *Ahh to heck with it*. I understood her totally. I remember coasting to a stop outside my house and just falling off my bike, even though I knew Dad was right behind me and my punishment for riding without a helmet would last forever—which it did.

Well, it lasted a month. Seemed like forever.

Stumbler landed with a bump, skid and tumble near an old barn. We spilled off her like french fries. You know, the field was not as soft as it looked from up in the air.

The little dragon stretched her full length. She gave a weird falling sigh then she breathed out. Flames played along her snout.

"Come on," said Izzy, grabbing hold of Dad's arm, pulling him to his feet. "Let's get out of here. That other dragon is coming!"

"Ouch," said Dad, freeing his burned hand.

We hustled over to the barn. It was empty and smelled like wood and sun. We ducked through the open doorway.

"The big dragon will know we're here. What if it comes after us?" said Izzy. "Should we run?"

The field outside was wide and flat, with no cover, not even a tree. The moon was high, bright, full. If we ran, we'd be as exposed as eggs in a frying pan.

"We'll be okay," I said. "The black dragon is after Stumbler, not us."

"It is?"

"That's what Stumbler thinks, anyway. I know what she's feeling."

"But how do you—what? *What?*"

Izzy stared at me. I shrugged.

"I just do," I said.

"That's a heckuva bump on your forehead, Buddy," said Dad. "Are you feeling okay?"

Seconds later the black dragon dropped from the sky. Sure enough, she ignored the barn completely, grabbing Stumbler's haunch in her two front claws. Roof-sized wings flapped slowly, powerfully, as she lifted off. I stepped out of the barn to watch. Stumbler hung upside down. Her head dangled near my eye level. I was close enough to see her blink and focus on me, then move her damaged forefoot. Was she waving good-bye? I want to think so. I waved back. The big dragon lifted her high, and took off across the moon.

We stood in the empty field in the moonlight, the three of us, safe for the first time. Izzy yawned wide enough to swallow a cantaloupe. Dad twisted himself around to crack his neck, like he does. The blur of dark stubble went all the way around his jaw. That reminded me.

"You used to have a beard," I said. "Didn't you have a beard?"

"Oh yeah—but that was years and years ago. Do you really remember, Buddy?"

I remembered getting lost in the insect gallery of the museum, looking at giant cockroaches with Izzy and Dad, and then looking away to find myself surrounded by strangers. The guy beside me had Dad's kind of pants, but his skin was darker and he didn't have a beard. Dad had left without me. I ran to the next room, and the one after that, scared I was getting farther away from him. When I heard his voice echoing up the marble stairwell, relief hit me like a hammer. And he wasn't even talking to me. "Hey there, Mrs. Solarski!" he said. "How are you doing? How's your lovely daughter?"

I ran toward him, crying. He picked me up, called me Buddy. I put my arms around his neck. His beard against my face was a familiar scratch. I'd been in danger and now I was safe. He turned me round and made me wave to Mrs. Solarski and her daughter Joanne. Not that we knew the Solarskis very well—they lived in the neighborhood and the family owned a drug store. But Dad did that kind of thing. A salesman remembers names, he liked to say.

We stopped at the candy store on the way home. *Why weren't you there?* I asked him. *Why did you go away? Why?*

These scenes were so clear now. Like a film. How come I couldn't remember any of them when I was talking to Dr. Nussbaum?

We walked through the field and subdivision toward the downtown, making plans. A phone so Dad could call home and arrange for money. That was the first thing. Then—then—

"We should go home too."

I think Izzy and I both said it at the same time.

"Well, yeah, of course," said Dad. "You'll be coming home with me when I—"

He stopped talking and walking too. Stood there a minute with his hands on his hips. We were out of the subdivision now, on a street with older houses, under a streetlight that flickered.

He took a deep inhale. "I can't help thinking you're my kids," he said.

He held out his arms and we both came over. He put his arms around us, squeezing carefully because of his bad hand.

"We *are* your kids," Izzy said. Her voice a bit muffled.

"Yeah," said Dad. "Yeah, you are. I wouldn't be here without you."

My heart felt too big for my chest, a pillow you pack into a suitcase and then can't close the lid on.

41

Remember the black dragon scorching the roof of that old building on main street? Now the building was on fire. It looked pretty serious too. Pumper truck, two police cars, ambulances, the whole thing. Lean yellow flames ran downward from the roof and had already reached the second floor when we got there. There was a crowd hanging around, mostly in pajamas. I realized the place wasn't a town hall. It was a hotel, advertising cheap rooms by the day, week or month, and it burned like a match.

A cop came over as soon as he saw us. He looked concerned as anything. "Come this way, please," he said. "I didn't see you before. You folks must have been on the top floor, eh?"

He led us to an ambulance, where a woman in uniform took charge of us. The badge on her sleeve said she was an EMT. Emergency something. She handed us breathing things without even asking our names.

I guess she thought we were hotel guests. A natural assumption, given the way we smelled and looked.

"You okay?" she said to me. "You want to lie down?"

When Dad held out his burned hand, the emergency-something woman got busy with sterile water and cream and a roll of bandages.

Izzy and I sat next to him. We didn't want to be out of touch. I mean we wanted to be able to touch him.

A woman wearing a breathing thing was on her phone, saying that she was on her way to the hospital in Lindsay. She lifted up her mask to talk, then dropped it to listen. That reminded me. I asked the emergency woman if I could borrow a phone to call home. She gave me her personal one, and I punched in the number.

"Hel-lo?"

I don't know why, but I assumed that Freddie would answer. The landline phones were in the kitchen and in Mom's room. Mom and Dad's I mean. Anyway, hearing Mom's tired voice was a real surprise.

"Hello? Hello?"

I couldn't ask to speak to Freddie and I couldn't say, *Hi, Mom.* "Stand by," I said. Dumb, but I don't know what I was thinking. My voice cracked on the last word—it hadn't done that in a while.

I handed the phone to Dad. "It's Mom," I whispered.

His face lightened, hearing me say it was her. He took the phone eagerly.

"Baby? That you?"

Izzy and I exchanged looks. His was sad. I guess mine was too.

"Listen, a lot has happened. Mostly good. Here's what's going on."

Dad explained where he was and what he wanted Mom to do. He sounded totally normal—like my dad, you know? I tried to work out why that made me so sad. He was the same guy. And he loved me. I believed that. Maybe it was hearing him tell his story as if I wasn't sitting beside him. "Yeah," he said, "there was an accident, and I'm going to the hospital in Lindsay. I'm okay, though. Yeah, up near Peterborough. You can come and get me there."

Dad was only here because of me and Izzy. This was our story and he was telling it like we weren't there. It was a kind of good-bye.

Was that it? Did I sense that this was good-bye, that I wouldn't see Dad again?

I didn't want that to be true. I didn't. I really didn't. I—

I didn't know.

Dad had Izzy on the phone now, saying he'd see her soon. The other Izzy—the one sitting beside him—muttered angrily. Was she mad at Dad or at her upside-down self, the Izzy who still had a father and who was still going out with Harry.

Dad's hand was bandaged now. The emergency woman left her phone with us and went to help somebody else.

"Bye bye, Puddin'," said Dad. "Put Freddie on."

"Let me talk to him," I said.

I waited until I heard his hello before saying anything.

"Hey, it's me, Freddie."

"Hey, wow!" He paused. "Great to hear from you, there, *Dad*. How you doing?"

There were a couple of crackles and murmurs, and then his voice came again, softer.

"Fred! It's you. And you found Dad. That is so cool!"

"Yeah."

"He was supposed to be home yesterday and he never even called. So you found him. That's great! You sure he's okay? He says they want to take him to the hospital. That sounds bad. What was it, an accident? Did you guys get in a crash or something? And how's Isabel—your Isabel, I mean. She's okay too?"

Freddie was a chatty guy, all right.

"She's fine," I said.

"You wanna talk to Casey? I'm in the back hall and he's here with me. You wanna say hi? Or you can see him tomorrow, I guess. Will you be coming?"

"I don't know," I said. "I don't know when I'll be around."

Pause.

"Well, whenever you do it'll be cool."

"Yeah," I said. "And give Casey a pat and a treat for me, okay? Hey, Dad knows about us. About my world I mean. We told him."

Freddie isn't stupid. "I guess so," he said. "If he was just talking to Izzy, and he asked for me, then he must know. Cool. Okay then."

"Okay then." I said it too.

I could feel Freddie grinning into the phone.

"Is it weird, being with him?"

I had to think for a second.

"No," I said. "Weird stuff has happened, but it's *amazing* to be with him."

"I got to ask, is he different from your own dad? I mean, I look like you, but we're different. Is it that way with him too?"

Of course, I never told Freddie about Dad. I'd blocked him out of my memory. I was there for Casey. Freddie thought I went home to the same family he had.

"He's my dad too," I said.

I gave back the phone. Izzy had hold of Dad's other hand, so for a second the three of us were connected, hand to hand to hand. It felt—I don't know—right. It was what we'd come for. I didn't want to let go.

When Dad lifted the phone to his ear his face lit up.

"Freddie! Hey Buddy!"

Izzy and I looked at each other. Nodded. Knew what we had to do.

Dad was saying something to his son. His other son. Izzy let go of his hand and we slipped away. They were sorting people into ambulances. We slid quietly to the edge of the crowd, took a couple of steps into shadow and kept walking.

"I'm tired," said Izzy. "It's like I'm carrying—"

"Everything," I said. "Yeah, I know."

We cut through two backyards to the next street, took a left and kept going. No talking—we both knew what was going on, what we were looking for. A couple of blocks later we got to the new subdivision. They were putting in sewers. Drainage ditches were open on one side of the street but filled in on the other. Stacks of plastic pipe shone under the streetlights.

Each house had a little tree in the front yard. A sapling. We stopped at a maple with dark leaves. You know how leaves are softer in the spring, like a baby's skin? Nice, isn't it?

"Should we have said good-bye to Daddy?"

"We don't have to."

I wouldn't have seen it if I hadn't been looking down. It. The light that came from our world. We'd got to the end of the block. The drainage ditch was deeper here. More of a hole than a ditch. I guess they needed extra room to put in pipes with a joint. Whatever, I was looking into the hole and there it was, faint but steady. A light.

"This is the place," I said.

"What if it doesn't work?" said Izzy. "What if we can't get home?"

"It'll work," I said.

We stood side by side, looking down. An automatic sprinkler overshot the lawn beside us, and our shoes were getting splashed.

"Don't cry," said Izzy.

"I'm not."

"Don't cry."

But she was crying herself.

A rabbit hopped out from behind a bush and stared at us for a moment before heading across the lawn in an easy rocking-horse motion.

"Look—a bunny," she sniffed.

The bell around its neck jingled softly. Not a wild rabbit. Someone's pet had escaped. I wished it luck.

I took the stick of deodorant out of my pants pocket. It had been there all along, a bit of Dad to bridge two worlds. Izzy still wore the shoes he'd bought her.

We held hands and leaped together.

42

I was sure we'd get home. I couldn't make sense of it or explain it—but so what? Belief is not about making sense. So when Izzy and I jumped into the drainage ditch with the light at the bottom, and kept going, I wasn't surprised. We fell through time, space, darkness, reality, whatever it is that connects worlds. Hands clasped tightly, in breathing silence, we fell.

There was still an inch of water in the Sorauren Park drain. The light I'd seen, looking down, hung from a metal pole in the middle of the park. It was brand-new, super bright. The park was boarded up. Hoardings all around it. We had to climb out of the place. The sign on the outside of the hoardings side said: COMING SOON—A GROUP 82 DEVELOPMENT. We stood on the sidewalk, clothes and hair and hands dripping.

"I feel like I weigh two hundred pounds," Izzy panted.

"But you don't feel upside down."

We walked the two blocks home. No lights in the houses, no cars, no pedestrians. No one around but us. The place seemed more unreal than the upside-down world.

Izzy thought the same thing. "So weird," she panted. "Is it us? Are we doing this?"

Elvira met us in the front hall. Her hair was a mess. She squeezed it with her hand and yawned wide.

"Good thing you decided to come back tonight," she said. "They put fences around Sorauren Park just after you left. I was scared they'd close off the drain too. I climbed over and lifted the top a bit for you. You won't be able to use that much longer, eh? Some kind of condo going in."

I showered first, changed clothes, came downstairs. Elvira had water on to boil.

The picture on the piano was almost as big as a sofa cushion. There was Dad, with his arm around Mom. Me and Izzy in front. All of us trying to look happy, dammit.

How had I been able to block it out, to not see it?

The metal frame rattled when I played a C major chord. No wonder I'd hated practicing.

The mind is amazing.

Izzy came down after her shower, in the bathrobe she never wore except when she was sick. We sat in the living room with all the lights on, sipping hot chocolate.

Elvira was in the small round chair with her legs tucked under her, peering at us intently.

"So you went down and met your dad, eh?"

We nodded.

"Bet you're tired. That time I saw Pushkin, I felt like I was carrying the world on my shoulders all the time I was down there. Drink your chocolate and go to bed. Don't worry about getting up. It's not a school day, and your mom isn't due until after dinner. What are you staring at, Fred?"

"Nothing."

The top of the piano, beside the picture. Nothing there now, but there used to be, didn't there? A vase kind of thing made out of blue glass, with a lid.

"Was it really an urn?" I whispered to Izzy. She nodded.

"What was in the urn?" asked Elvira.

Neither of us said anything.

"Oh."

Mom pulled two *J'aime Montreal* T-shirts from her purse and tossed them at me and Izzy, poured herself a glass of wine and walked around the kitchen telling us about her plane rides and hotel room and the people she'd met. She thought we should all go to Montreal some time. "I learned a lot and I was only there for two days," she said. "It's Canada, but it's not like here. The same but different—you know?"

She grabbed my chin and turned my head.

"What happened, honey? Looks like somebody hit you. Did you get in another fight?"

I shook my head.

"Accident," I said.

"With a human fist?"

"Dragon tail."

"Well, I guess it's okay if you can make a joke about it. But seriously, you're not in trouble, are you? Fred? Are you?"

"Seriously, no."

My clock said 2:15. I got up and went next door.

"Izzy," I whispered.

"Yeah?"

"You awake?"

"Yeah."

The streetlight shone through her window. Her face looked pale and blotchy, and her eyes were extra dark.

"I had a nightmare," I whispered.

"Me too."

"Or maybe it wasn't a nightmare. But I felt bad when I woke up. Dad was alive. He was okay. He smiled and waved at me. And—and then he was gone."

Izzy wore her Bart Simpson nightie. I had a T-shirt and sweatpants with a rip up one leg that Mom wouldn't let me wear outside. I sat on her bed. She scooted over to make room for me.

"Maybe it was all a dream," she said.

"Huh? What?"

"The whole day. Or a story, you know? Something we told each other. A dream we both had."

I thought about that. I thought about it all being a story, happy and sad, fun and not fun, the way stories are. Freddie and Casey and the basketball game. The trucker lady from the Windy City. Stumbler the dragon. Dad calling me Buddy.

"What if—"

I stopped.

"Yeah?"

"What if it isn't a story. What if it's real, that world down there. But only because of us up here."

"You and me? Elvira was there too."

"Anyone can get there. It's a real world, but you have to *will* it into life. We found Dad, because we miss him. He's alive because of us. Anyone can get to this world if they miss someone enough. And that's why," I was talking louder now, "that's why we were so tired. Willpower is hard. Concentrating on something tires you out. What did Elvira say—she felt she had the weight of the world on her."

"He's still dead," Izzy said.

She'd known all along, while I was still hung up about Casey. She was smarter than me. Or braver.

"What is it, Fred?"

I shook my head. She sat up and put her arms around me. I was crying. I tried to tell her, but the words stuck. And then she was crying too. We sat on her bed in the middle of the night and held each other and cried for the longest damn time.

"When I was seeing Dr. Nussbaum," Izzy said, "he told me to—"

"I didn't know you saw him."

"Sure. Mom did too. Anyway, he said one way to get my feelings out and connect with Daddy was to write him a letter. You know, *Dear Daddy, I miss you so much. Every day I wake up thinking I will see you, and then I remember that I will not see you today, or tomorrow, or ever again* . . . that kind of thing."

I wiped my face. "Did you do it?"

"Uh-huh. I showed it to the doctor, and we put it in an envelope addressed just *Daddy*, and he stuck a stamp on it and we walked to the mailbox and mailed it off."

I was frowning by now. "It didn't get to him."

"Duh."

Lights flashed across the ceiling as a car drove down Wright Avenue. Izzy's window was open a little, so we could hear the sound of the tires on the wet street.

"Dad's dead up here," I said. "But not down there."

"But—so what? If the world is only in our mind—"

"And Elvira's. And who knows how many others. It's real. The bruise on my face—Mom noticed. The green hoodie is not mine, it's Freddie's."

"Are you sure? It looks like something you'd—"

"And people die down there. Don't forget the dragons."

I sat up straight and made fists.

"Think about that world, Izzy. No one worries there—the dragon comes and takes them away and no one cries or fights. *We* care up here. That place exists in our imaginations, in our willpower. That's the link."

"And the dragons break the link."

"Yeah. I mean, maybe."

"Yeah. They take you away when it's your time. When no one thinks about you anymore. When no one misses you."

I thought about the dragons hovering over the volcano. I could imagine not missing a piano or a swing set anymore. But a dragon had dropped that old man in. Because no one missed him?

"Ewww," I said.

"Maybe not," said Izzy. "I don't know."

"So let's not break the link with Dad," I said.

We both laughed but it was kind of a sob too. Whatever you call that.

"Daddy was going to die down there," Izzy whispered a minute later.

"Right. He's alive because we saved him."

"I drove the car. I pushed him onto the dragon's back."

There was a huge gob of saliva inside me. I choked and swallowed and choked some more. Izzy leaned forward and wiped my face with her sleeve.

"He called us his kids," she said. "Remember? He knew where we were from and he still called us his kids. He's down there, but he really is our dad."

Izzy pulled the spread to cover me and gave me one of her pillows. We lay quiet while our breathing slowed down. I remembered Dr. Nussbaum asking if there was someone I wanted to write to. Okay then, what would I put in a letter?

Dear Dad. That was as far as I got. It didn't make me feel any closer to him. Izzy was asleep. She rolled toward me and put a warm hand on my shoulder That helped. My thoughts started to go all drifty, like soap bubbles floating around the bathtub. Velma on the classroom floor. Lisa on the telephone. Frogs in the toilet tank. Toes on the front bumper. I smiled. That last one was from Linda Mae, the trucker.

I decided not to bother with a long letter to Dad. I'd just give him the trucker's farewell.

All the good numbers.

ACKNOWLEDGMENTS

Trust your key readers. It's your story, but they see things you don't. The first one to see a draft of this was Miriam Toews, who was so enthusiastic I persevered even when the going got sticky. Gayle Friesen was encouraging and candid, and wants to put a dragon in her next book. Thanks to Hilary McMahon for reading positively and selling hard. Huge thanks to Tara Walker for reading generously and critically. And passing the manuscript on to Lara Hinchberger, who was as thorough and careful as a lottery player with a maybe winning ticket. I trusted you all, and the story is better for it.

RICHARD SCRIMGER is the award-winning author of twenty books for children and adults. His works have been translated into many languages and have been critically acclaimed around the world. His first children's novel, *The Nose from Jupiter*, won the 10th Annual Mr. Christie's Book Award. His novel *From Charlie's Point of View* was a CLA Honour Book and was chosen as one of the Chicago Public Library "Best of the Best." Richard's latest, *Viminy Crowe's Comic Book*, was listed as a Top Shelf Honoree by *VOYA* magazine. His books *Ink Me* and *The Wolf and Me* are part of the Seven series with six other well-known authors. He lives in Toronto, Ontario. Visit him at scrimger.ca